CHICAGOLAND DETECTIVE AGENCY
N°3

Night of the Living Dogs

TRINA ROBBINS
ILLUSTRATED BY TYLER PAGE

GRAPHIC UNIVERSE™ • MINNEAPOLIS • NEW YORK

STORY BY **TRINA ROBBINS**

PENCILS AND INKS BY **TYLER PAGE**

LETTERING BY **ZACK GIALLONGO**

Graphic Universe™
A division of Lerner Publishing Group, Inc.
241 First Avenue North
Minneapolis, MN 55401 U.S.A.

Website address: www.lernerbooks.com

Main body text set in CC Wild Words.
Typeface provided by Comicraft Design.

Library of Congress Cataloging-in-Publication Data

Robbins, Trina.
        Night of the living dogs / by Trina Robbins ; illustrated by Tyler Page.
            p. cm. — (Chicagoland Detective Agency ; #03)
        Summary: When Megan, Raf, and talking dog Bradley get their first real case, they find themselves tracking a puppy that is not as adorable as it seems, and trying to end an ancient curse.
        ISBN: 978-0-7613-4616-6 (lib. bdg. : alk. paper)
        1. Graphic novels. [1. Graphic novels. 2. Dogs—Fiction.
3. Shapeshifting—Fiction. 4. Blessing and cursing—Fiction. 5. Japanese Americans—Fiction. 6. Science fiction.] I. Page, Tyler, 1976– ill. II. Title.
PZ7.7.R632Nig 2012
741.5'973—dc22   2011001031

Manufactured in the United States of America
1 – BC – 12/31/11

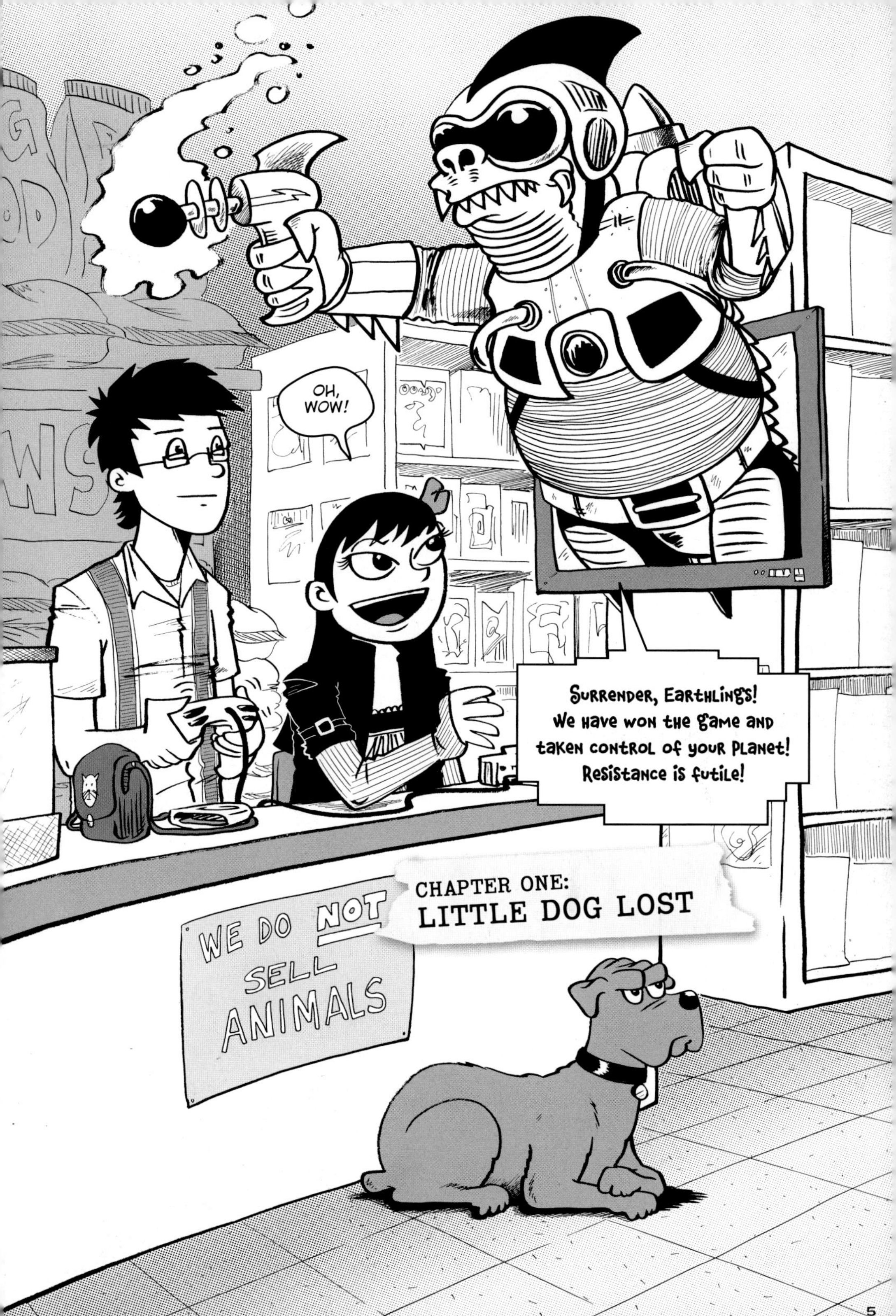
OH, WOW!
Surrender, Earthlings! We have won the game and taken control of your planet! Resistance is futile!
CHAPTER ONE:
LITTLE DOG LOST
WE DO NOT SELL ANIMALS

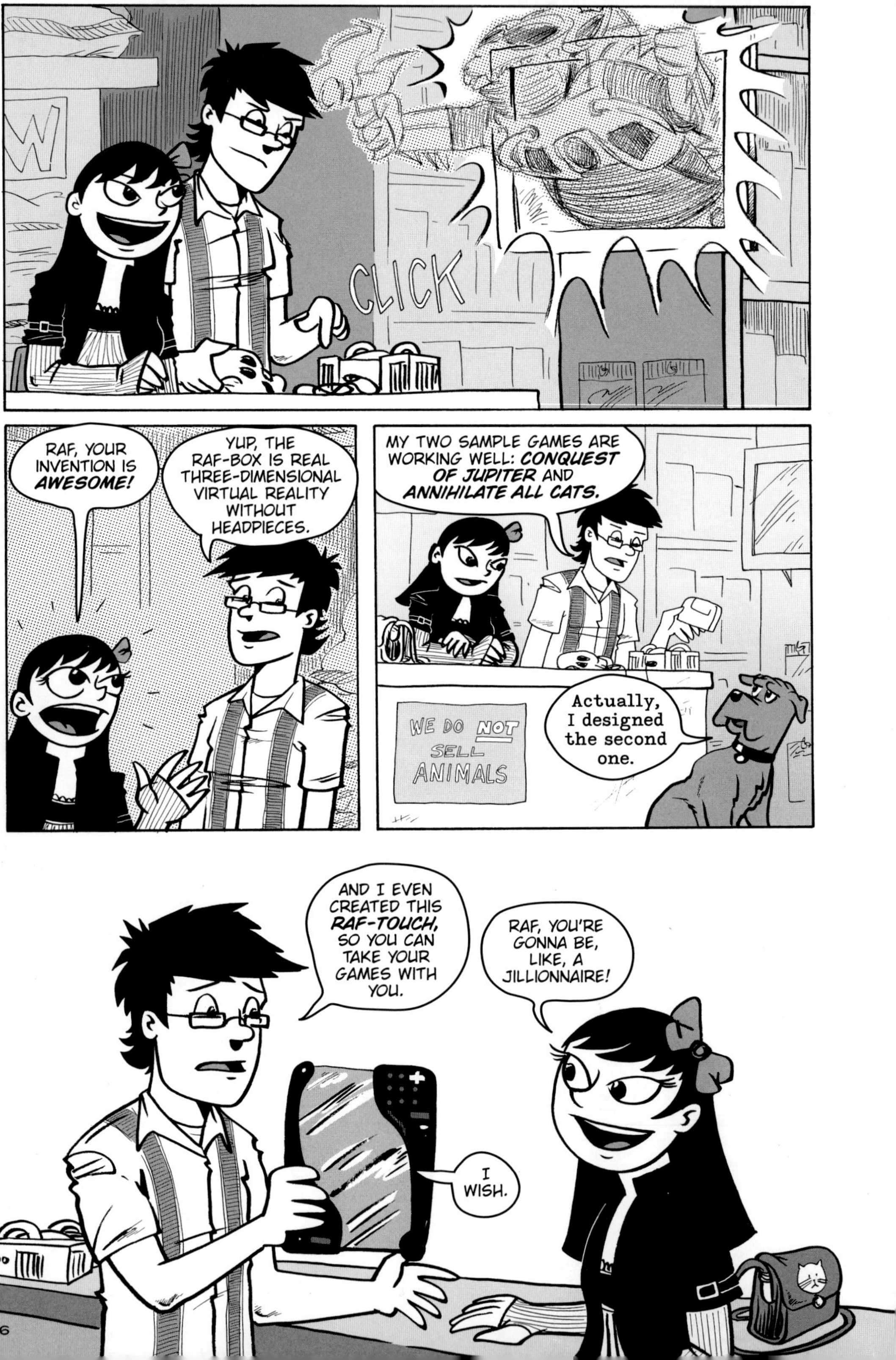
CLICK
RAF, YOUR INVENTION IS AWESOME!
YUP, THE RAF-BOX IS REAL THREE-DIMENSIONAL VIRTUAL REALITY WITHOUT HEADPIECES.
MY TWO SAMPLE GAMES ARE WORKING WELL: CONQUEST OF JUPITER AND ANNIHILATE ALL CATS.
WE DO NOT SELL ANIMALS
Actually, I designed the second one.
AND I EVEN CREATED THIS RAF-TOUCH, SO YOU CAN TAKE YOUR GAMES WITH YOU.
RAF, YOU'RE GONNA BE, LIKE, A JILLIONNAIRE!
I WISH.

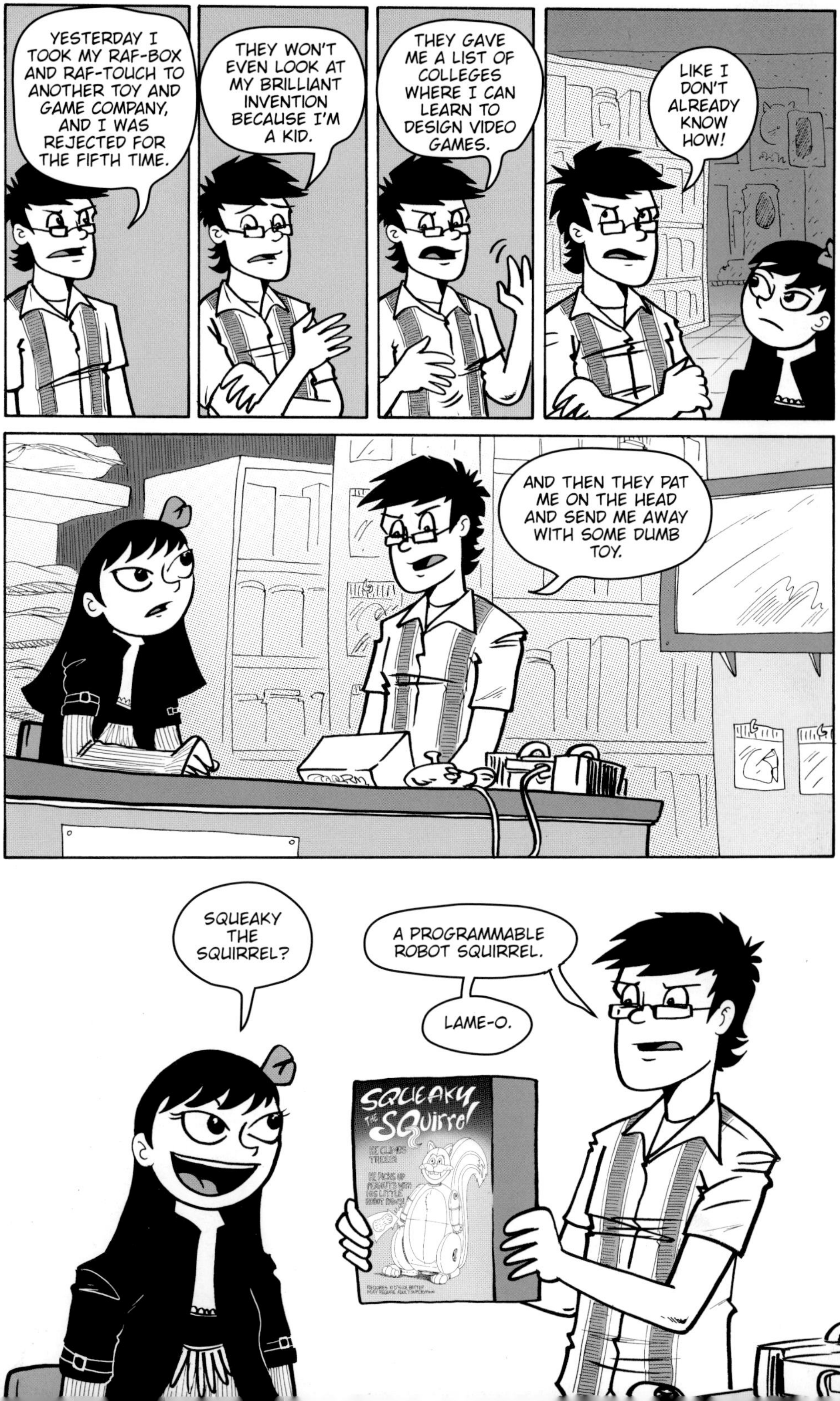
YESTERDAY I TOOK MY RAF-BOX AND RAF-TOUCH TO ANOTHER TOY AND GAME COMPANY, AND I WAS REJECTED FOR THE FIFTH TIME.
THEY WON'T EVEN LOOK AT MY BRILLIANT INVENTION BECAUSE I'M A KID.
THEY GAVE ME A LIST OF COLLEGES WHERE I CAN LEARN TO DESIGN VIDEO GAMES.
LIKE I DON'T ALREADY KNOW HOW!
AND THEN THEY PAT ME ON THE HEAD AND SEND ME AWAY WITH SOME DUMB TOY.
SQUEAKY THE SQUIRREL?
A PROGRAMMABLE ROBOT SQUIRREL.
LAME-O.
SQUEAKY THE SQUIRREL

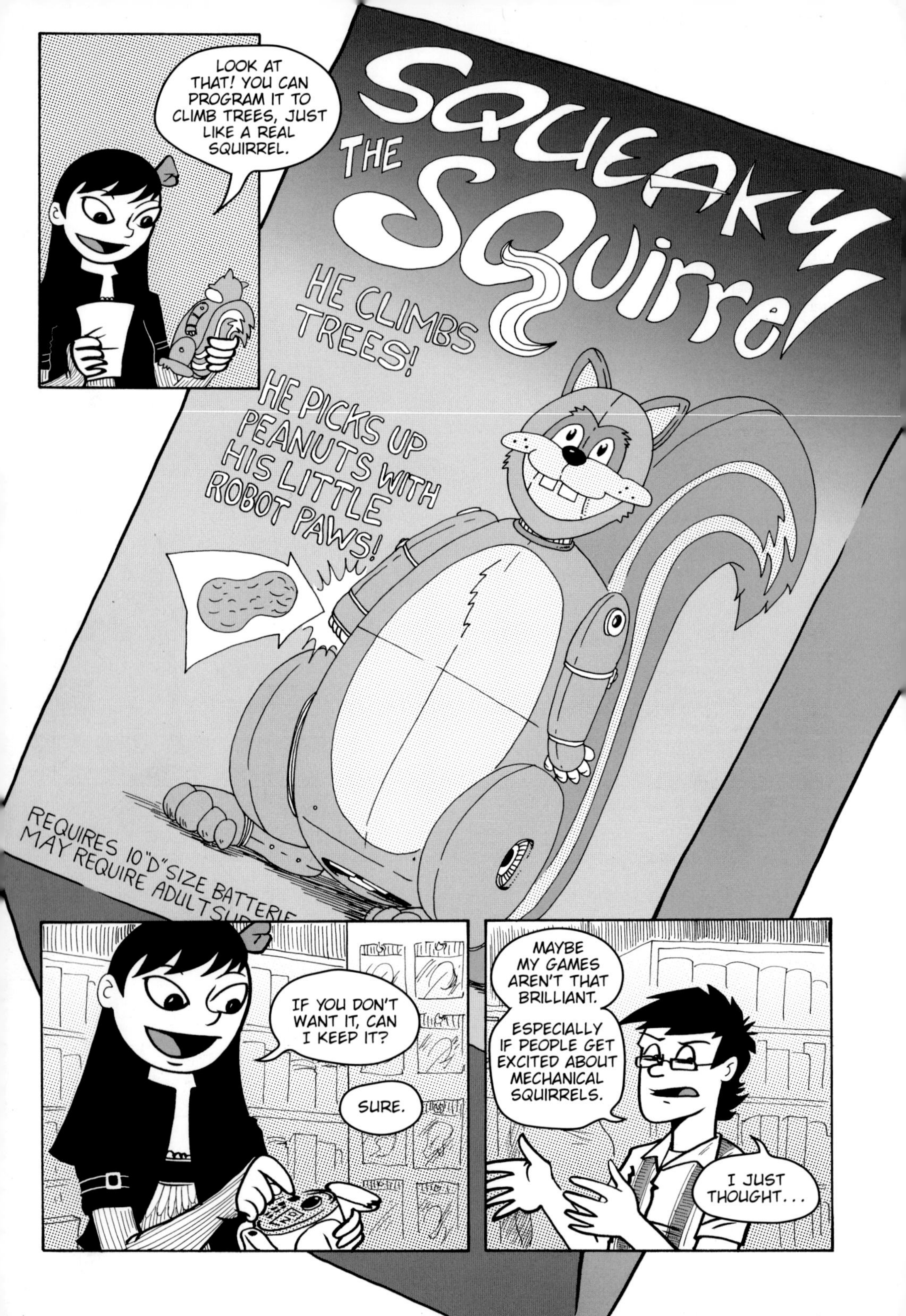
LOOK AT THAT! YOU CAN PROGRAM IT TO CLIMB TREES, JUST LIKE A REAL SQUIRREL.
THE SQUEAKY SQUIRREL
HE CLIMBS TREES!
HE PICKS UP PEANUTS WITH HIS LITTLE ROBOT PAWS!
REQUIRES 10"D"SIZE BATTERIE
MAY REQUIRE ADULTSU
IF YOU DON'T WANT IT, CAN I KEEP IT?
SURE.
MAYBE MY GAMES AREN'T THAT BRILLIANT.
ESPECIALLY IF PEOPLE GET EXCITED ABOUT MECHANICAL SQUIRRELS.
I JUST THOUGHT. . .

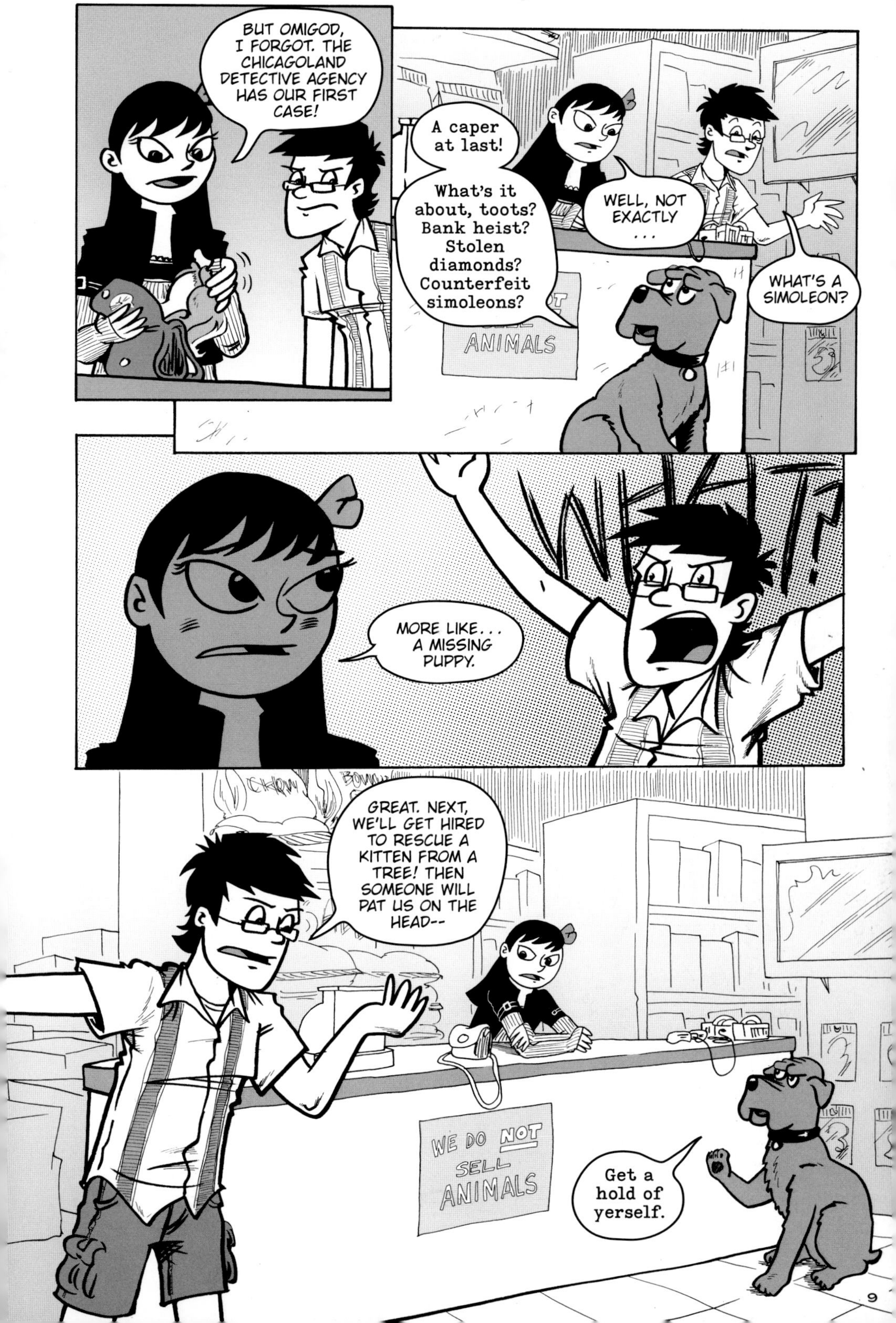
BUT OMIGOD, I FORGOT. THE CHICAGOLAND DETECTIVE AGENCY HAS OUR FIRST CASE!
A caper at last!
What's it about, toots? Bank heist? Stolen diamonds? Counterfeit simoleons?
WELL, NOT EXACTLY . . .
WHAT'S A SIMOLEON?
ANIMALS
WHAT?!
MORE LIKE . . . A MISSING PUPPY.
GREAT. NEXT, WE'LL GET HIRED TO RESCUE A KITTEN FROM A TREE! THEN SOMEONE WILL PAT US ON THE HEAD--
WE DO NOT SELL ANIMALS
Get a hold of yerself.

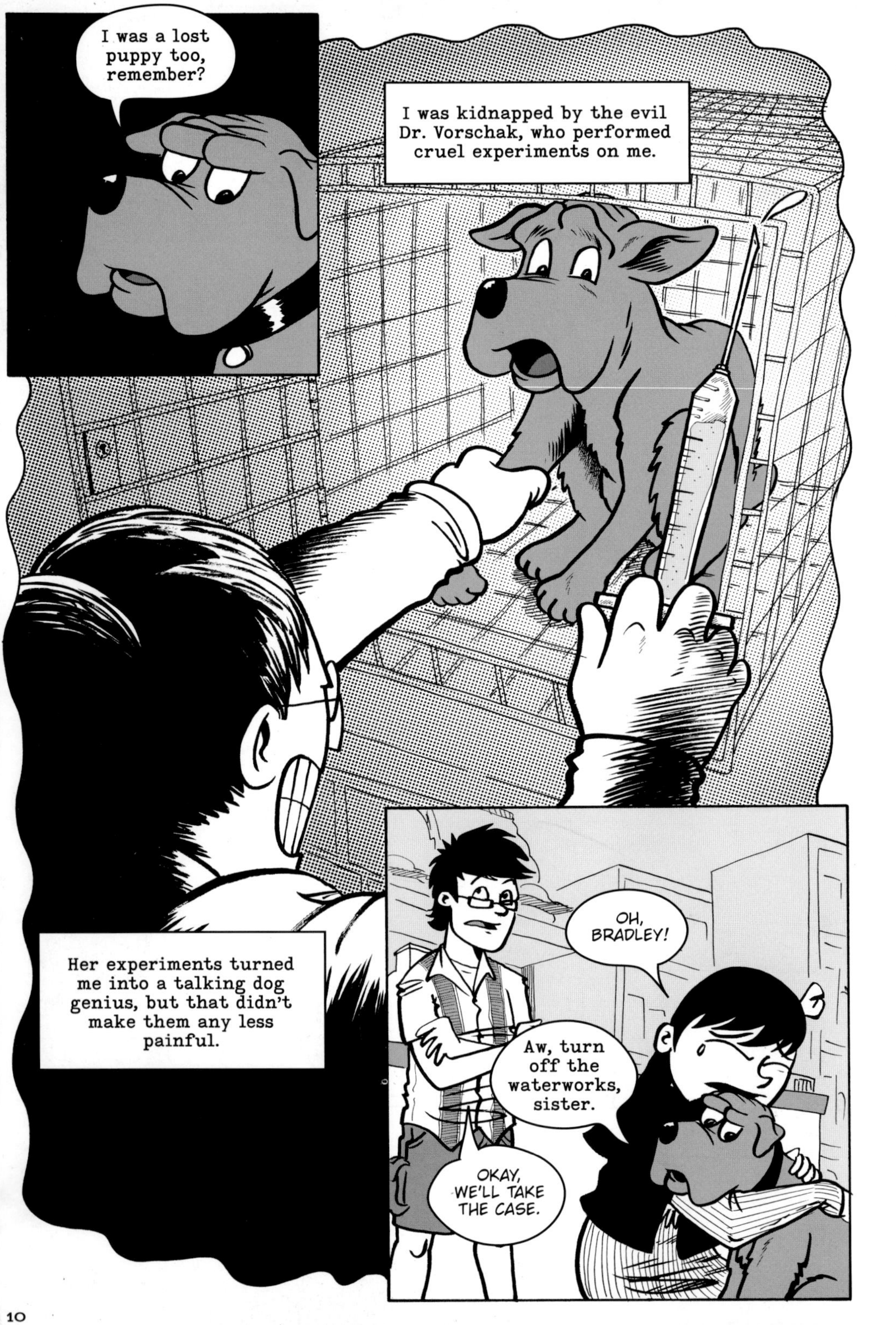
I was a lost puppy too, remember?
I was kidnapped by the evil Dr. Vorschak, who performed cruel experiments on me.
Her experiments turned me into a talking dog genius, but that didn't make them any less painful.
OH, BRADLEY!
Aw, turn off the waterworks, sister.
OKAY, WE'LL TAKE THE CASE.

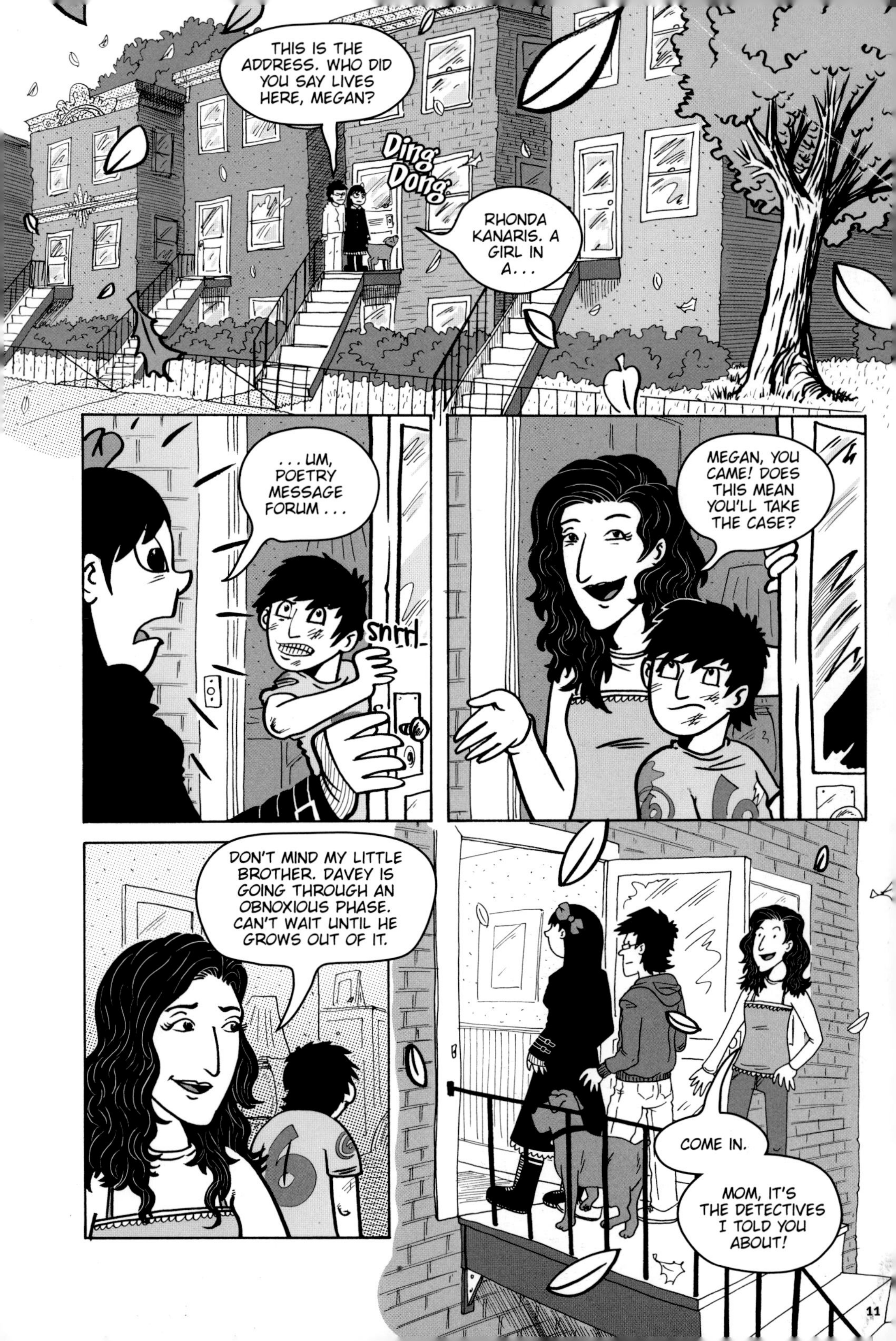
THIS IS THE ADDRESS. WHO DID YOU SAY LIVES HERE, MEGAN?
Ding Dong
RHONDA KANARIS. A GIRL IN A . . .
. . . UM, POETRY MESSAGE FORUM . . .
snrrl
MEGAN, YOU CAME! DOES THIS MEAN YOU'LL TAKE THE CASE?
DON'T MIND MY LITTLE BROTHER. DAVEY IS GOING THROUGH AN OBNOXIOUS PHASE. CAN'T WAIT UNTIL HE GROWS OUT OF IT.
COME IN.
MOM, IT'S THE DETECTIVES I TOLD YOU ABOUT!

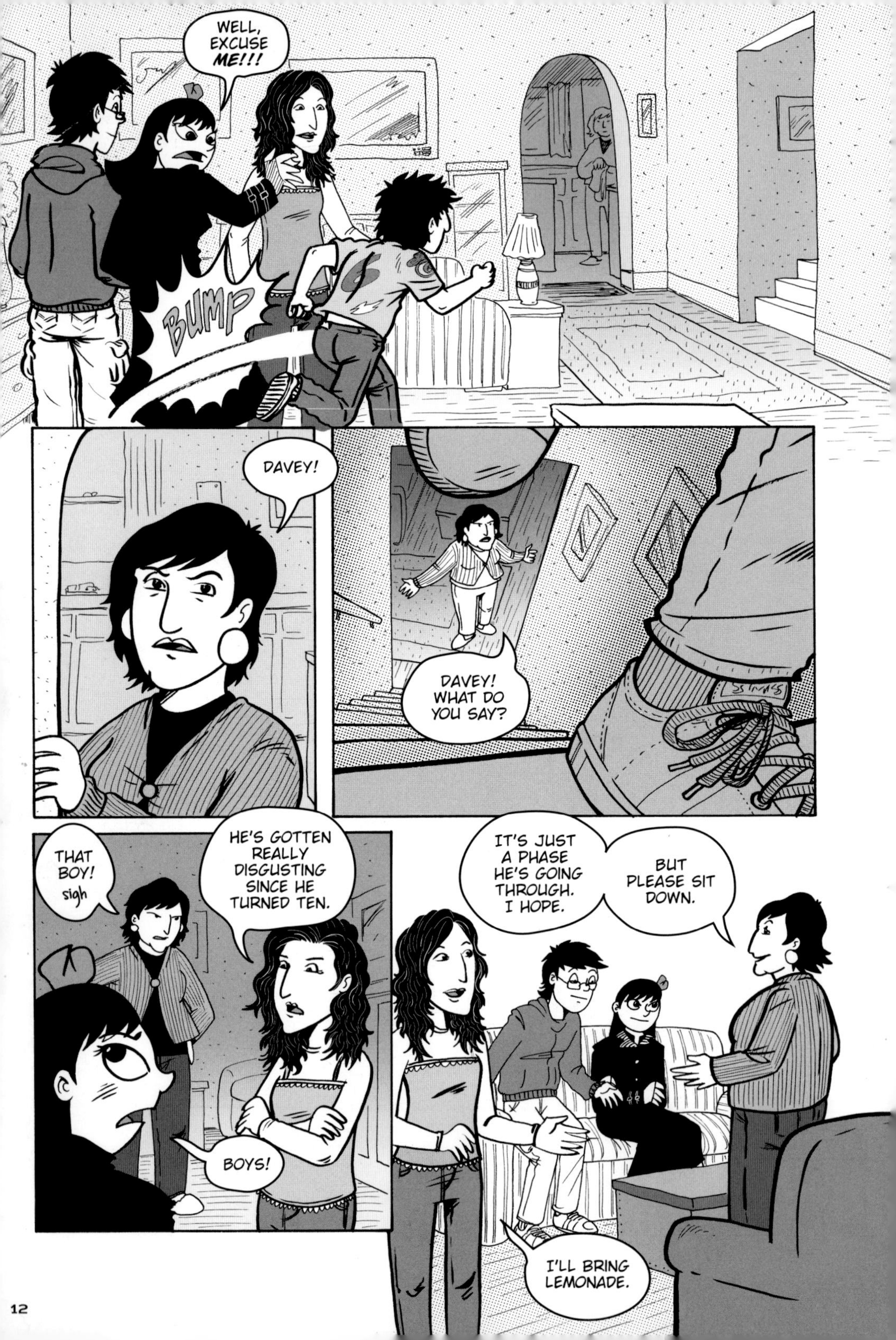
WELL, EXCUSE ME!!!
BUMP
DAVEY!
DAVEY! WHAT DO YOU SAY?
THAT BOY! sigh
HE'S GOTTEN REALLY DISGUSTING SINCE HE TURNED TEN.
BOYS!
IT'S JUST A PHASE HE'S GOING THROUGH. I HOPE.
BUT PLEASE SIT DOWN.
I'LL BRING LEMONADE.

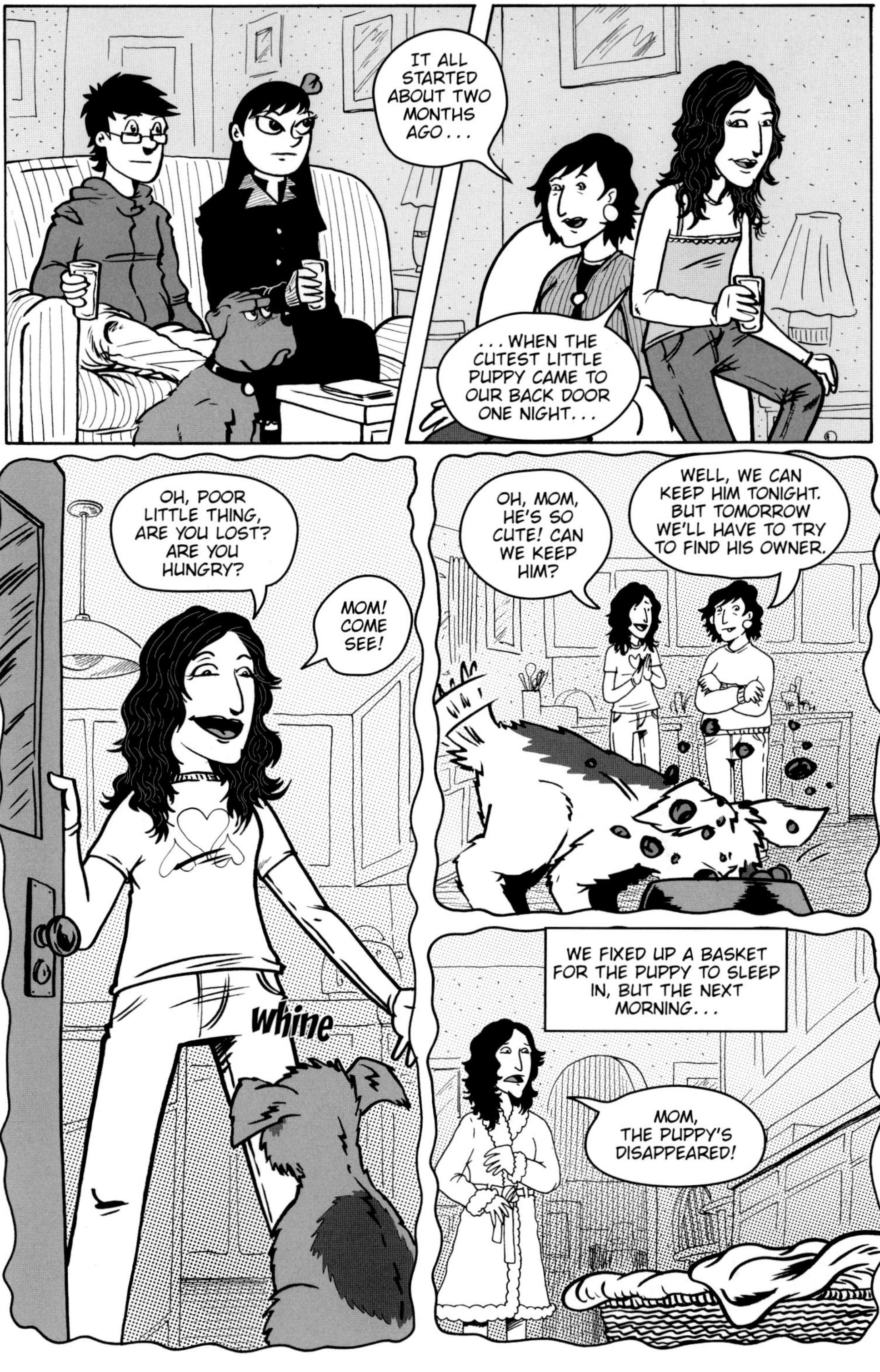
IT ALL STARTED ABOUT TWO MONTHS AGO...
...WHEN THE CUTEST LITTLE PUPPY CAME TO OUR BACK DOOR ONE NIGHT...
OH, POOR LITTLE THING, ARE YOU LOST? ARE YOU HUNGRY?
MOM! COME SEE!
whine
OH, MOM, HE'S SO CUTE! CAN WE KEEP HIM?
WELL, WE CAN KEEP HIM TONIGHT. BUT TOMORROW WE'LL HAVE TO TRY TO FIND HIS OWNER.
WE FIXED UP A BASKET FOR THE PUPPY TO SLEEP IN, BUT THE NEXT MORNING...
MOM, THE PUPPY'S DISAPPEARED!

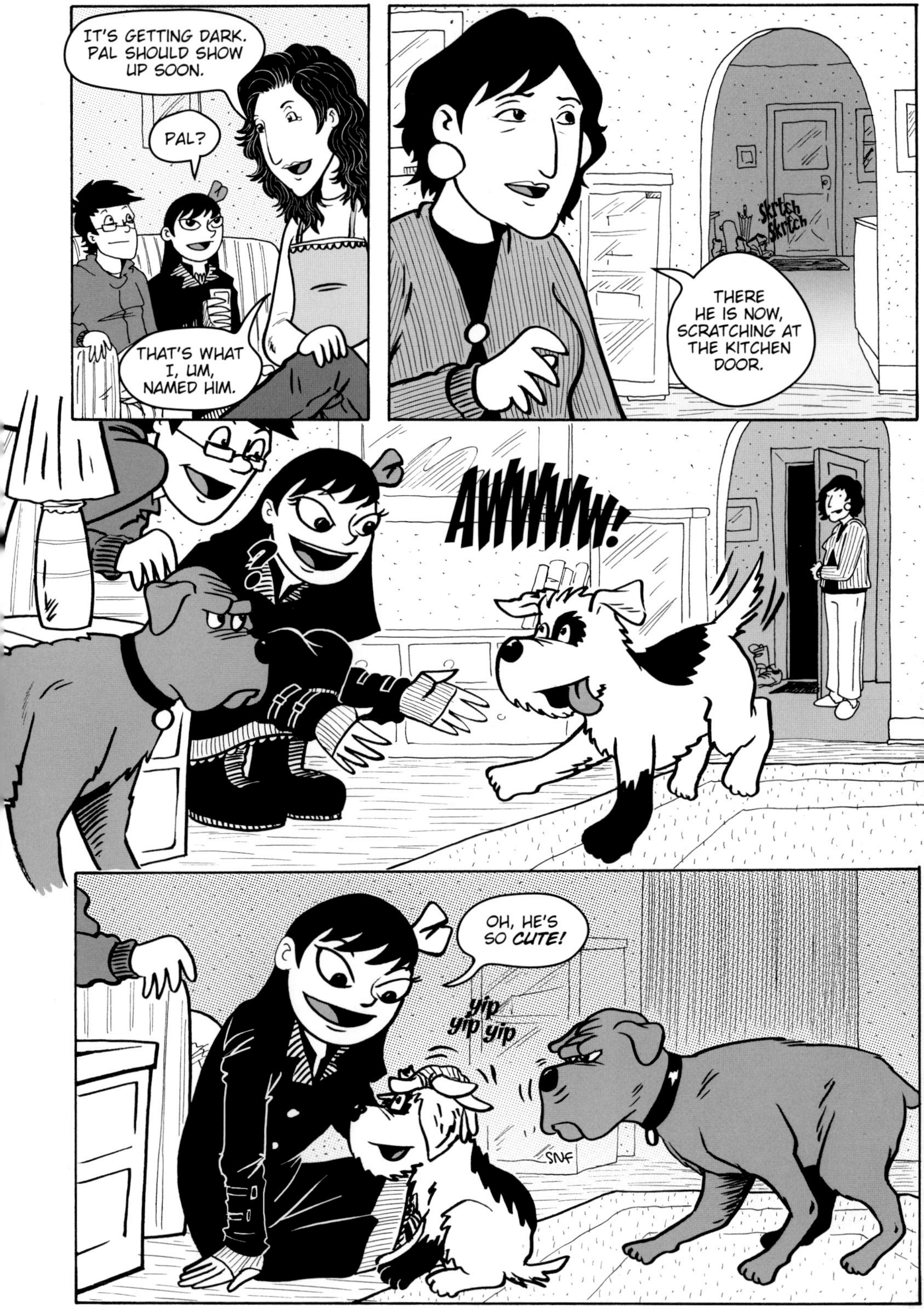
IT'S GETTING DARK. PAL SHOULD SHOW UP SOON.
PAL?
THAT'S WHAT I, UM, NAMED HIM.
Skrtsh Skrtch
THERE HE IS NOW, SCRATCHING AT THE KITCHEN DOOR.
AWWWW!
OH, HE'S SO *CUTE!*
yip yip yip
SNF

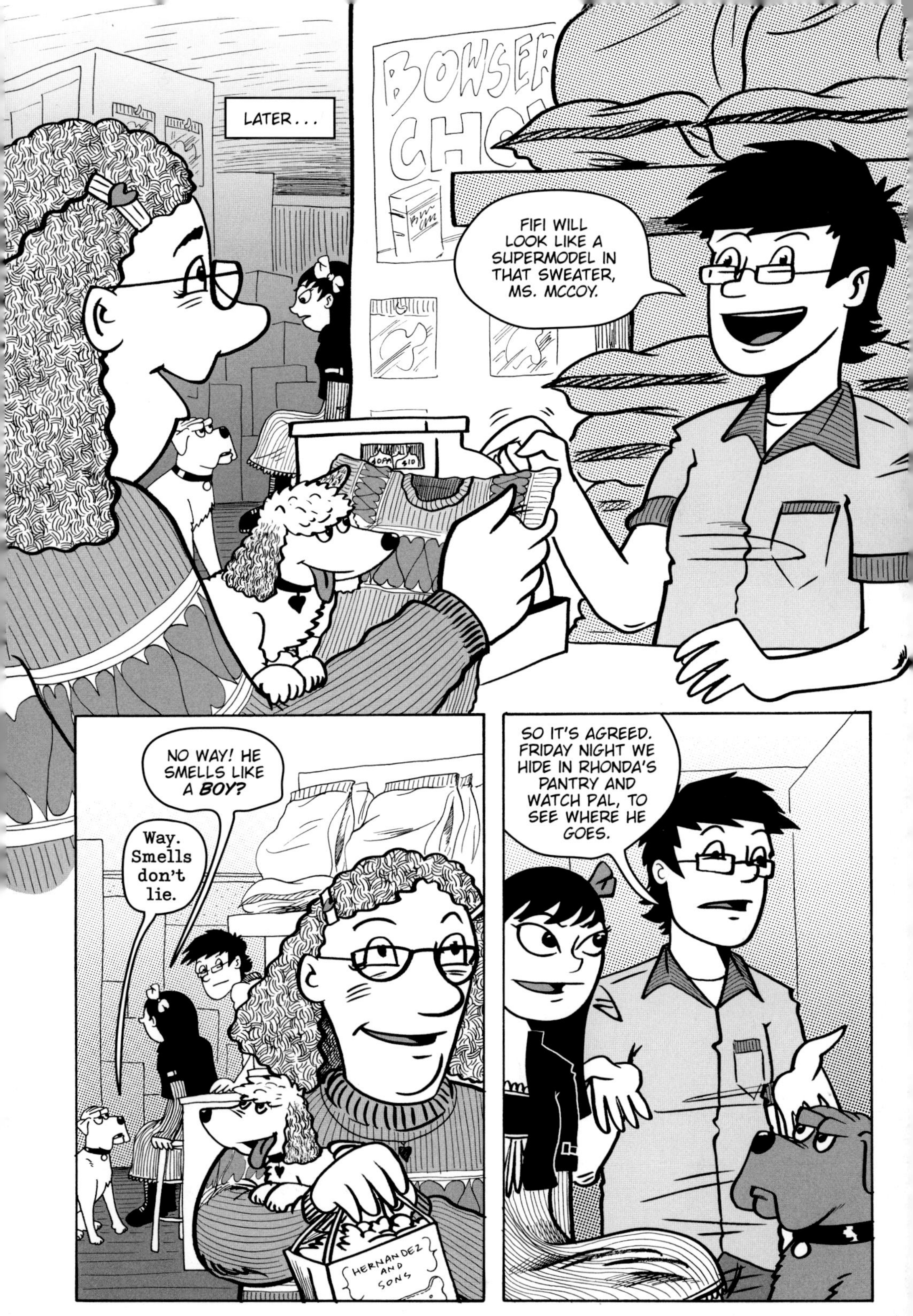
LATER...
BOWSER CHO
FIFI WILL LOOK LIKE A SUPERMODEL IN THAT SWEATER, MS. MCCOY.
NO WAY! HE SMELLS LIKE A *BOY?*
Way. Smells don't lie.
HERNANDEZ AND SONS
SO IT'S AGREED. FRIDAY NIGHT WE HIDE IN RHONDA'S PANTRY AND WATCH PAL, TO SEE WHERE HE GOES.

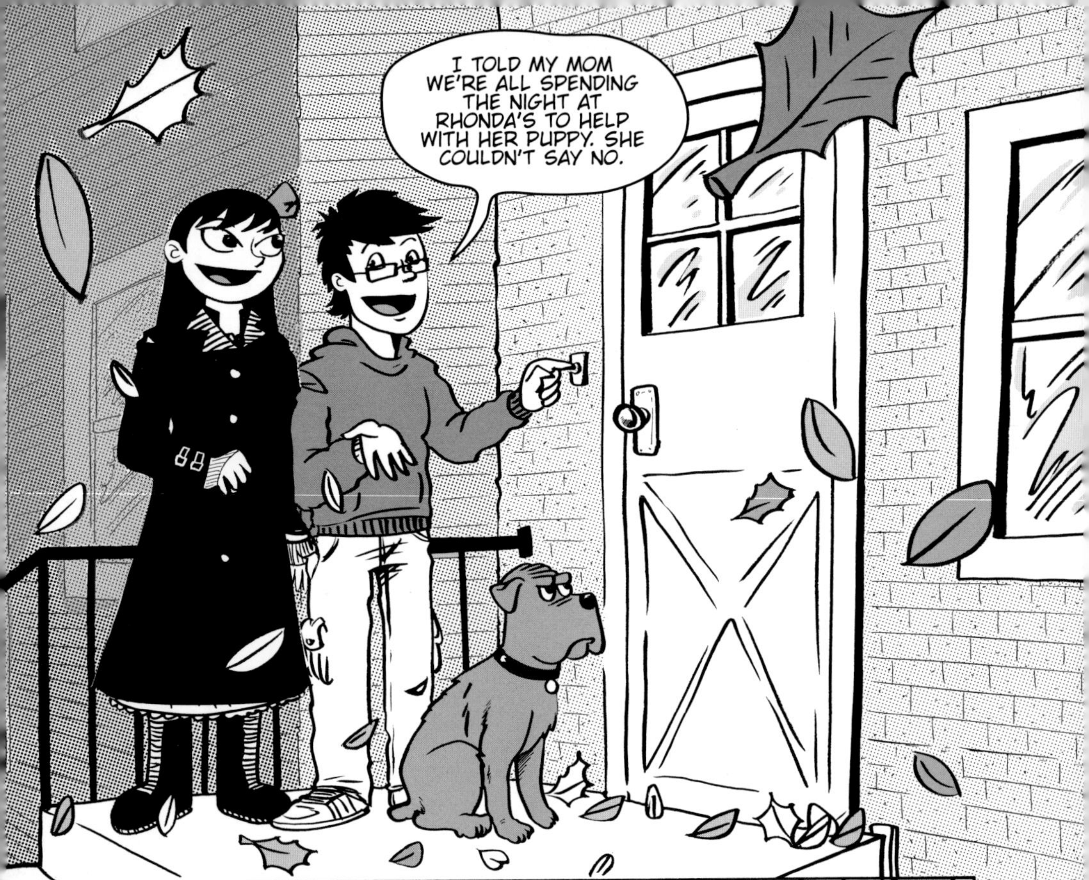
I TOLD MY MOM WE'RE ALL SPENDING THE NIGHT AT RHONDA'S TO HELP WITH HER PUPPY. SHE COULDN'T SAY NO.
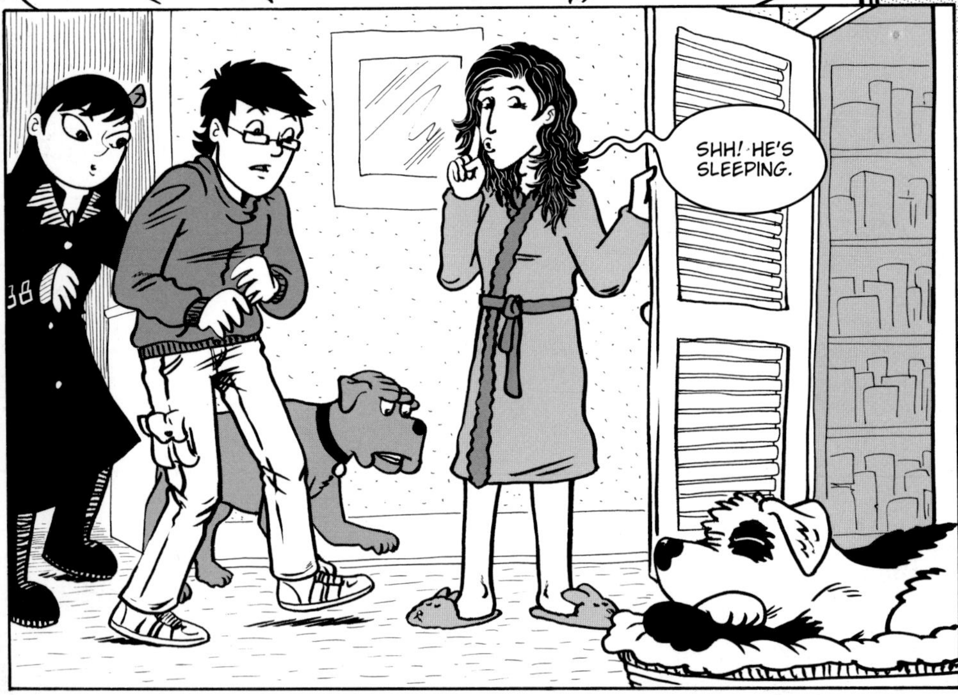
SHH! HE'S SLEEPING.

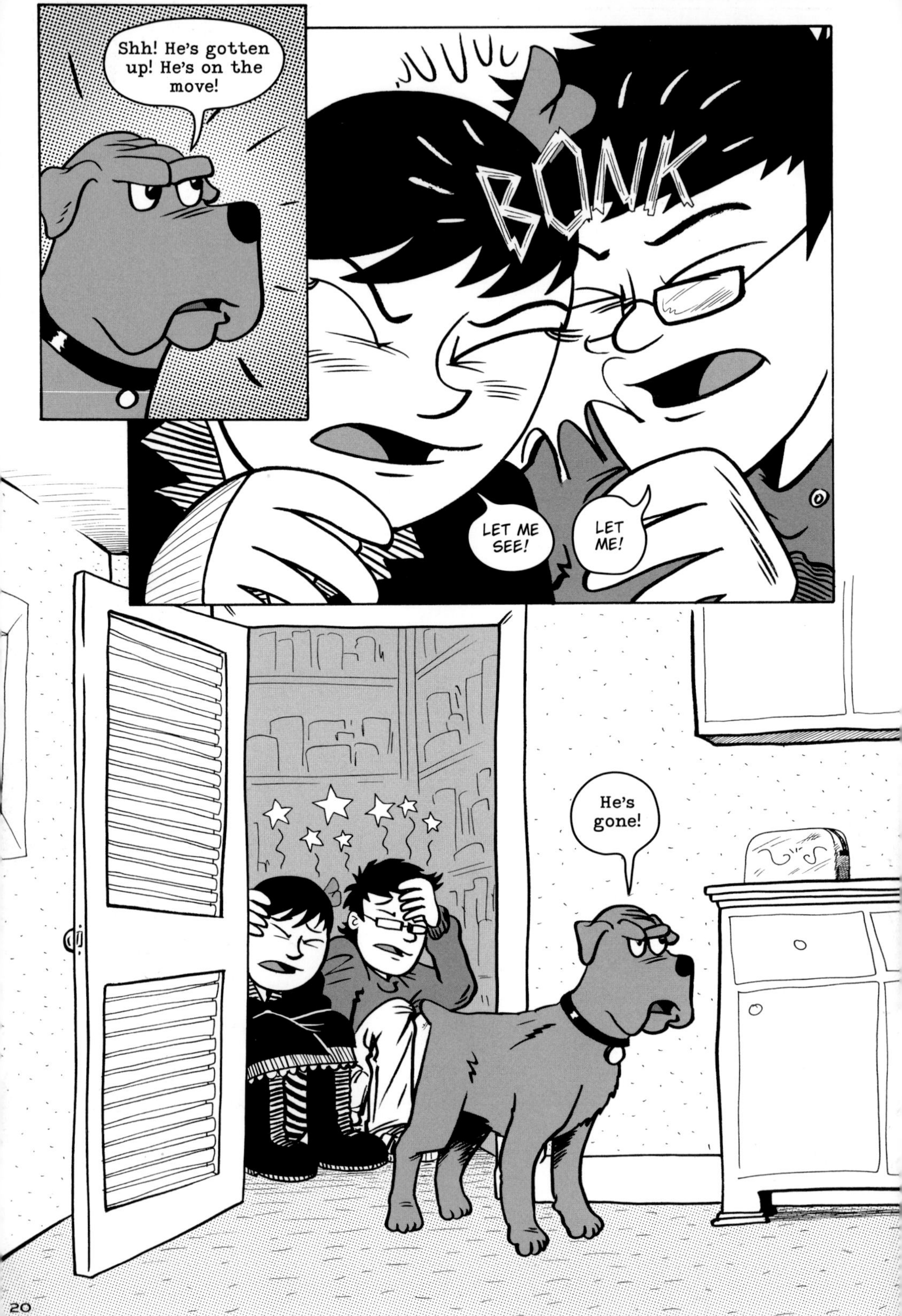
Shh! He's gotten up! He's on the move!
BONK
LET ME SEE!
LET ME!
He's gone!

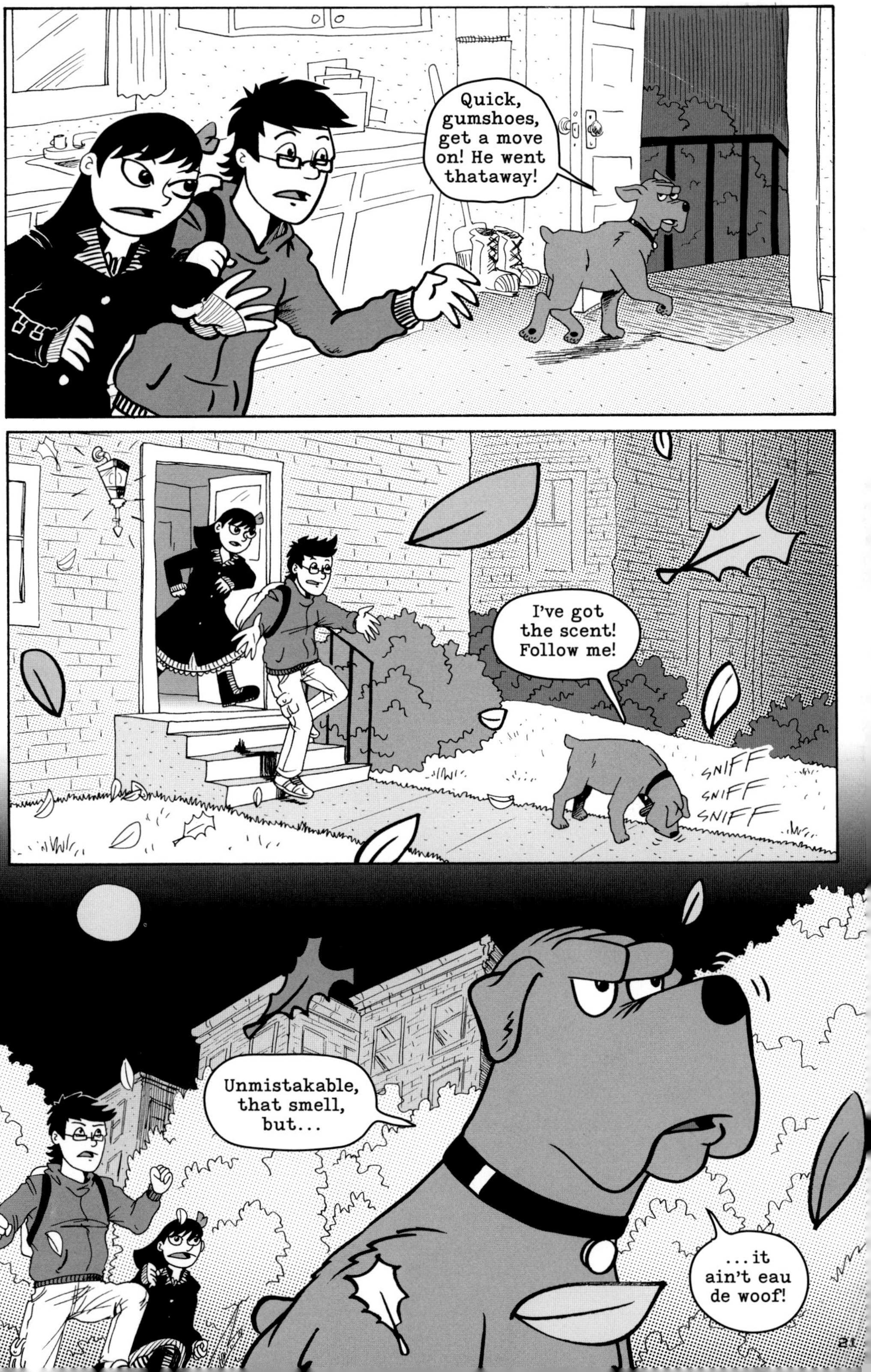
Quick, gumshoes, get a move on! He went thataway!
I've got the scent! Follow me!
SNIFF SNIFF SNIFF
Unmistakable, that smell, but...
...it ain't eau de woof!

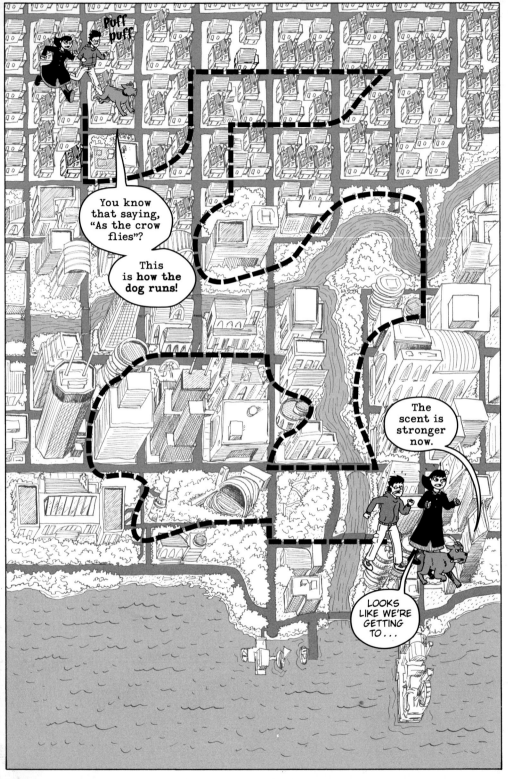

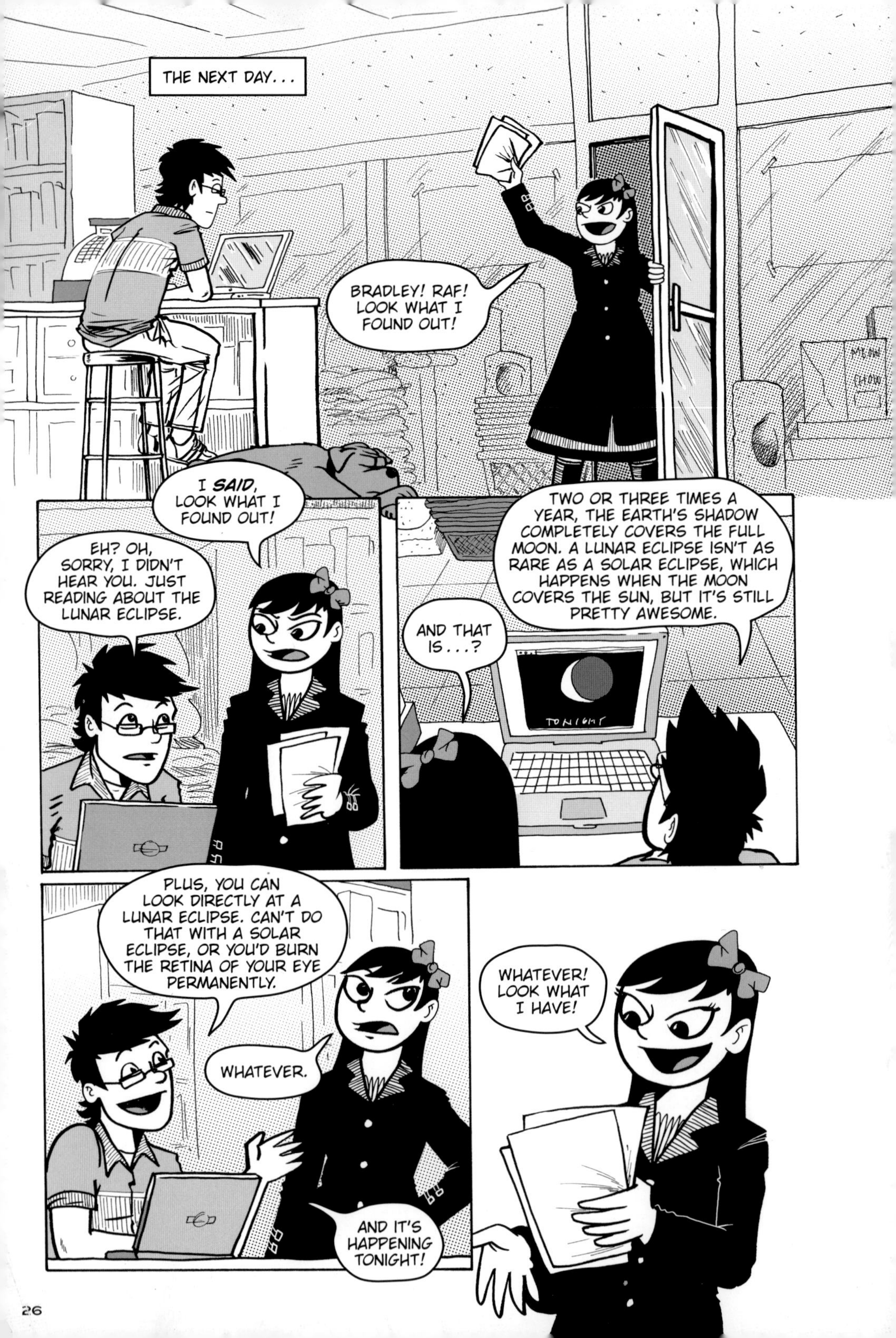
THE NEXT DAY...
BRADLEY! RAF! LOOK WHAT I FOUND OUT!
I SAID, LOOK WHAT I FOUND OUT!
EH? OH, SORRY, I DIDN'T HEAR YOU. JUST READING ABOUT THE LUNAR ECLIPSE.
AND THAT IS...?
TWO OR THREE TIMES A YEAR, THE EARTH'S SHADOW COMPLETELY COVERS THE FULL MOON. A LUNAR ECLIPSE ISN'T AS RARE AS A SOLAR ECLIPSE, WHICH HAPPENS WHEN THE MOON COVERS THE SUN, BUT IT'S STILL PRETTY AWESOME.
TONIGHT
PLUS, YOU CAN LOOK DIRECTLY AT A LUNAR ECLIPSE. CAN'T DO THAT WITH A SOLAR ECLIPSE, OR YOU'D BURN THE RETINA OF YOUR EYE PERMANENTLY.
WHATEVER.
AND IT'S HAPPENING TONIGHT!
WHATEVER! LOOK WHAT I HAVE!

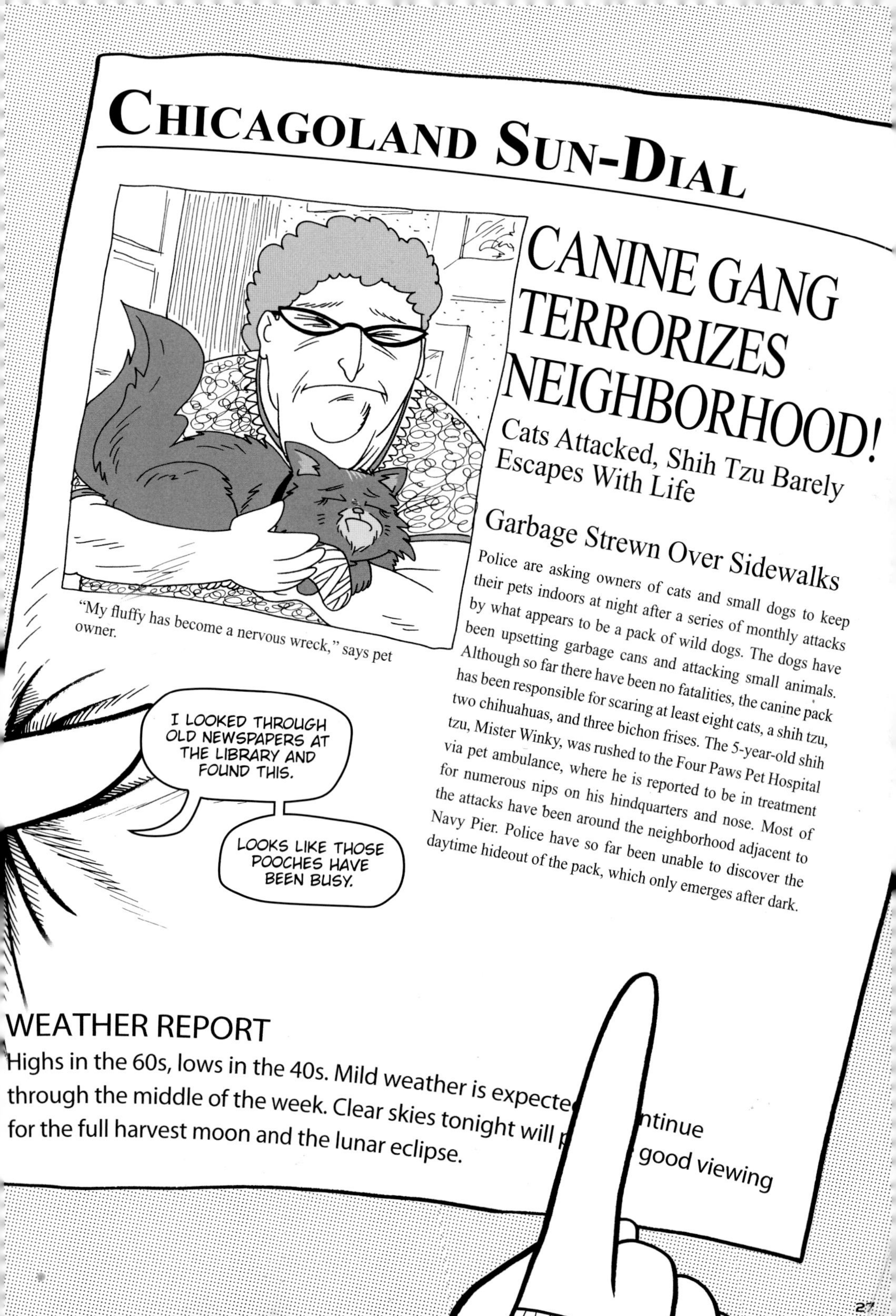

CHICAGOLAND SUN-DIAL
CANINE GANG TERRORIZES NEIGHBORHOOD!
Cats Attacked, Shih Tzu Barely Escapes With Life
Garbage Strewn Over Sidewalks
Police are asking owners of cats and small dogs to keep their pets indoors at night after a series of monthly attacks by what appears to be a pack of wild dogs. The dogs have been upsetting garbage cans and attacking small animals. Although so far there have been no fatalities, the canine pack has been responsible for scaring at least eight cats, a shih tzu, two chihuahuas, and three bichon frises. The 5-year-old shih tzu, Mister Winky, was rushed to the Four Paws Pet Hospital via pet ambulance, where he is reported to be in treatment for numerous nips on his hindquarters and nose. Most of the attacks have been around the neighborhood adjacent to Navy Pier. Police have so far been unable to discover the daytime hideout of the pack, which only emerges after dark.
"My fluffy has become a nervous wreck," says pet owner.
WEATHER REPORT
Highs in the 60s, lows in the 40s. Mild weather is expecte
ntinue
through the middle of the week. Clear skies tonight will p
good viewing
for the full harvest moon and the lunar eclipse.
I LOOKED THROUGH OLD NEWSPAPERS AT THE LIBRARY AND FOUND THIS.
LOOKS LIKE THOSE POOCHES HAVE BEEN BUSY.

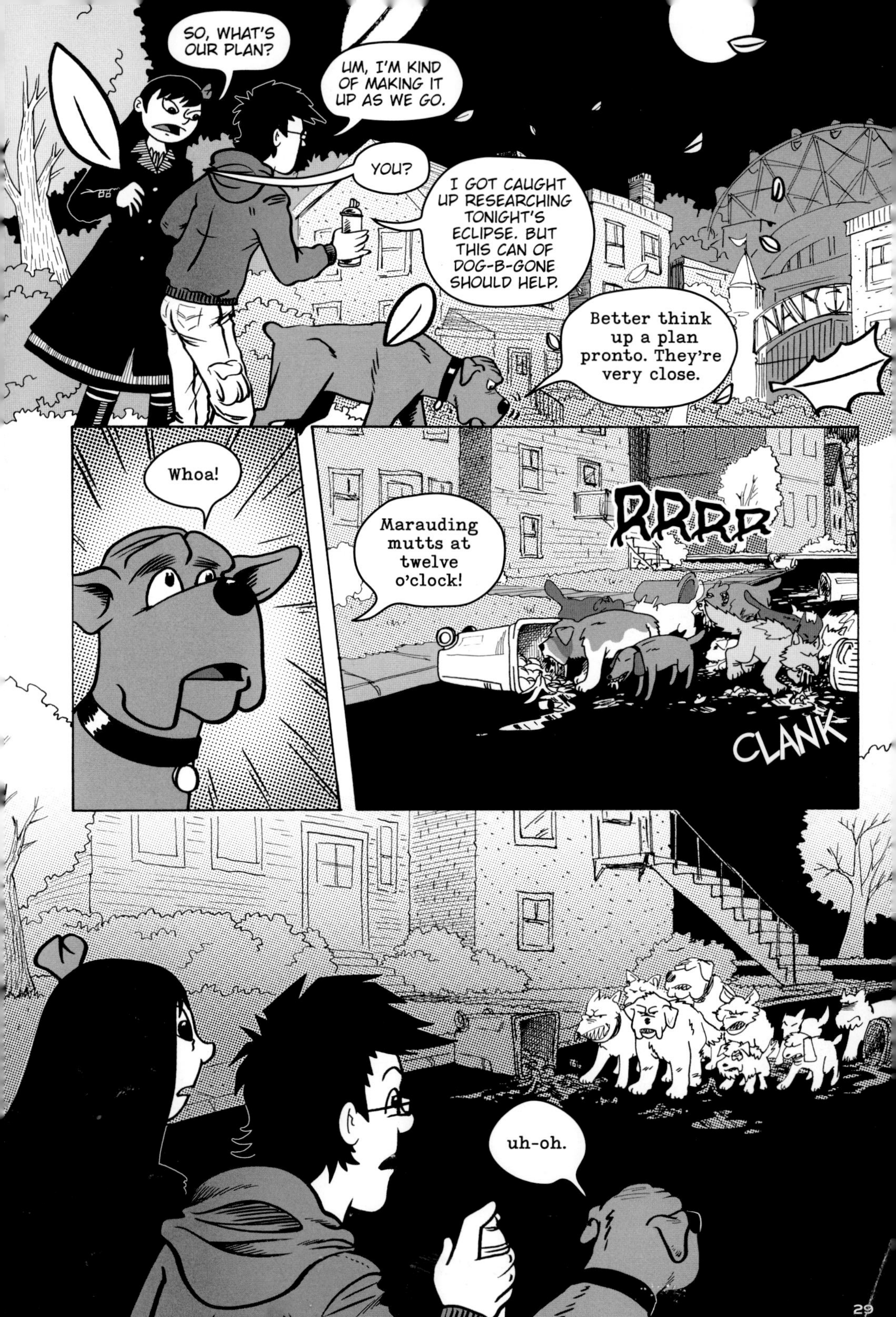

SO, WHAT'S OUR PLAN?
UM, I'M KIND OF MAKING IT UP AS WE GO.
YOU?
I GOT CAUGHT UP RESEARCHING TONIGHT'S ECLIPSE. BUT THIS CAN OF DOG-B-GONE SHOULD HELP.
Better think up a plan pronto. They're very close.
Whoa!
Marauding mutts at twelve o'clock!
RRRR
CLANK
uh-oh.

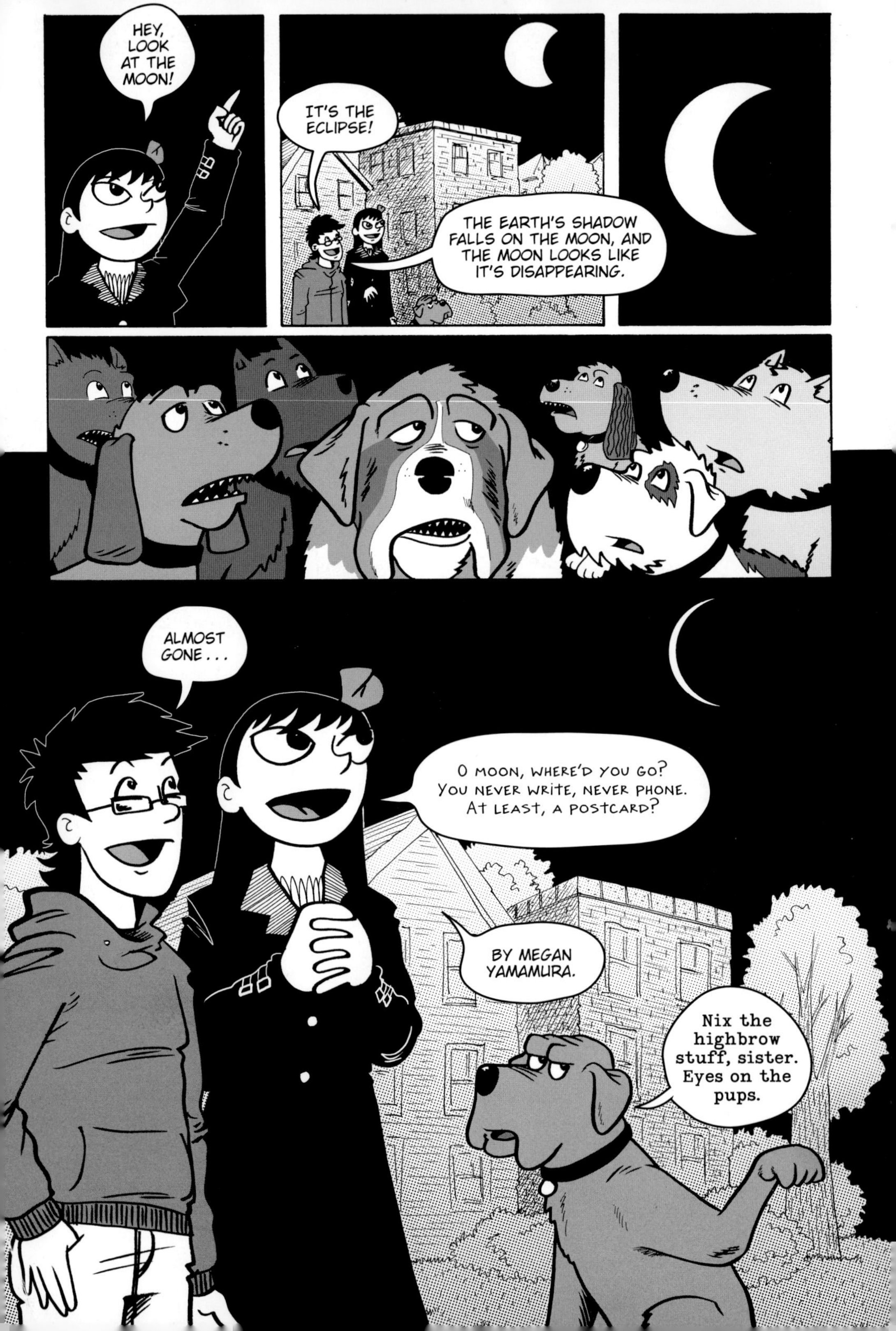
HEY, LOOK AT THE MOON!
IT'S THE ECLIPSE!
THE EARTH'S SHADOW FALLS ON THE MOON, AND THE MOON LOOKS LIKE IT'S DISAPPEARING.
ALMOST GONE . . .
O MOON, WHERE'D YOU GO? YOU NEVER WRITE, NEVER PHONE. AT LEAST, A POSTCARD?
BY MEGAN YAMAMURA.
Nix the highbrow stuff, sister. Eyes on the pups.

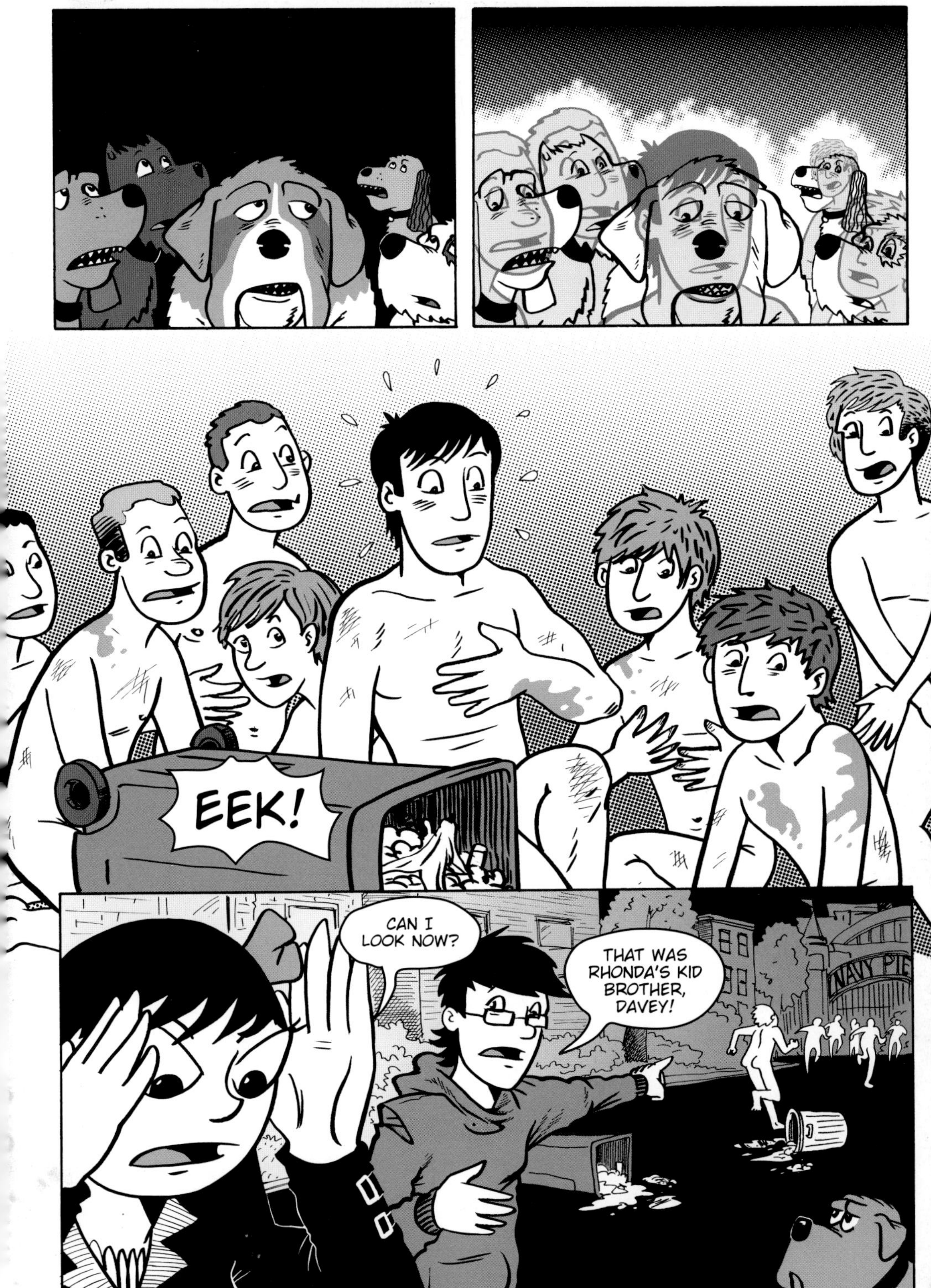
EEK!
CAN I LOOK NOW?
THAT WAS RHONDA'S KID BROTHER, DAVEY!

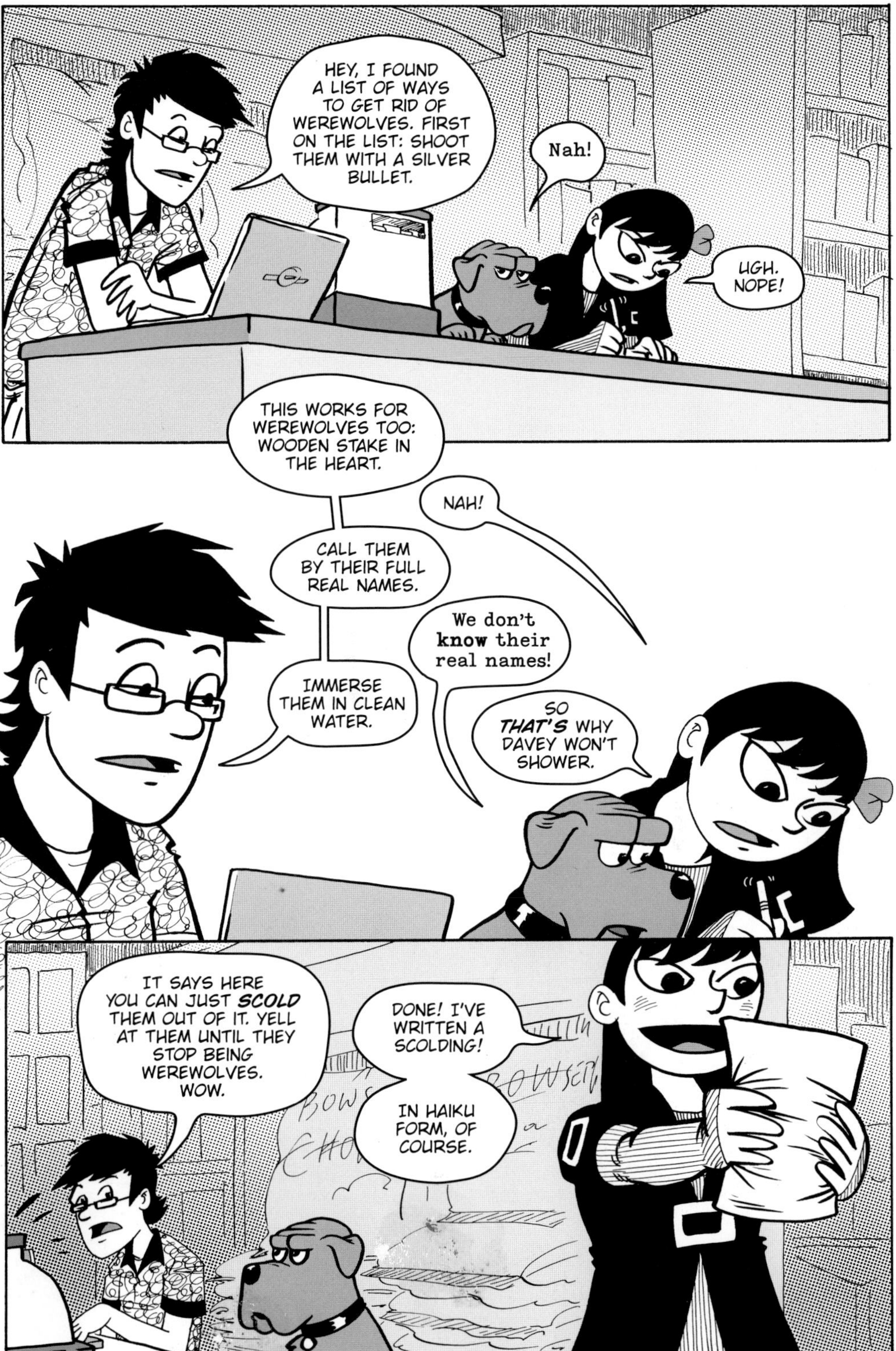
HEY, I FOUND A LIST OF WAYS TO GET RID OF WEREWOLVES. FIRST ON THE LIST: SHOOT THEM WITH A SILVER BULLET.
Nah!
UGH. NOPE!
THIS WORKS FOR WEREWOLVES TOO: WOODEN STAKE IN THE HEART.
NAH!
CALL THEM BY THEIR FULL REAL NAMES.
We don't **know** their real names!
IMMERSE THEM IN CLEAN WATER.
SO *THAT'S* WHY DAVEY WON'T SHOWER.
IT SAYS HERE YOU CAN JUST *SCOLD* THEM OUT OF IT. YELL AT THEM UNTIL THEY STOP BEING WEREWOLVES. WOW.
DONE! I'VE WRITTEN A SCOLDING!
IN HAIKU FORM, OF COURSE.

CHAPTER THREE:
THEREBY HANGS A TAIL
LYCAON? I KNOW THAT NAME FROM GREEK MYTHOLOGY.
The Lycaon
LYCAON WAS AN ANCIENT GREEK KING.

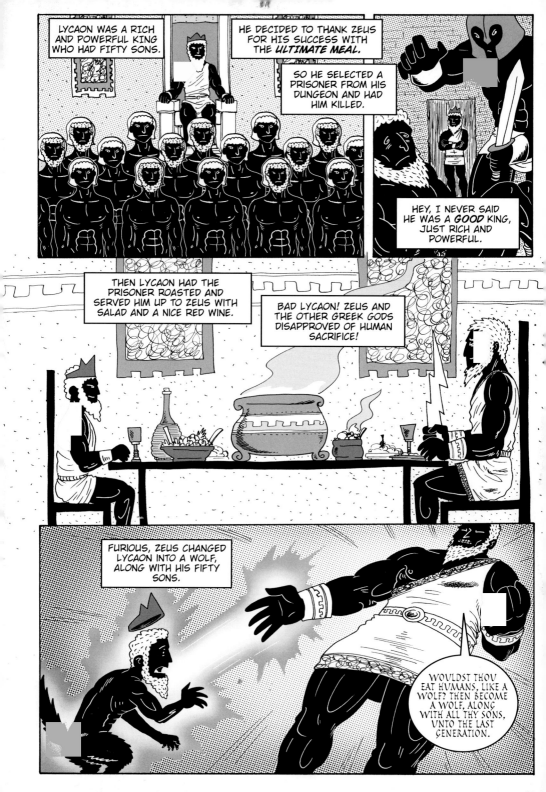

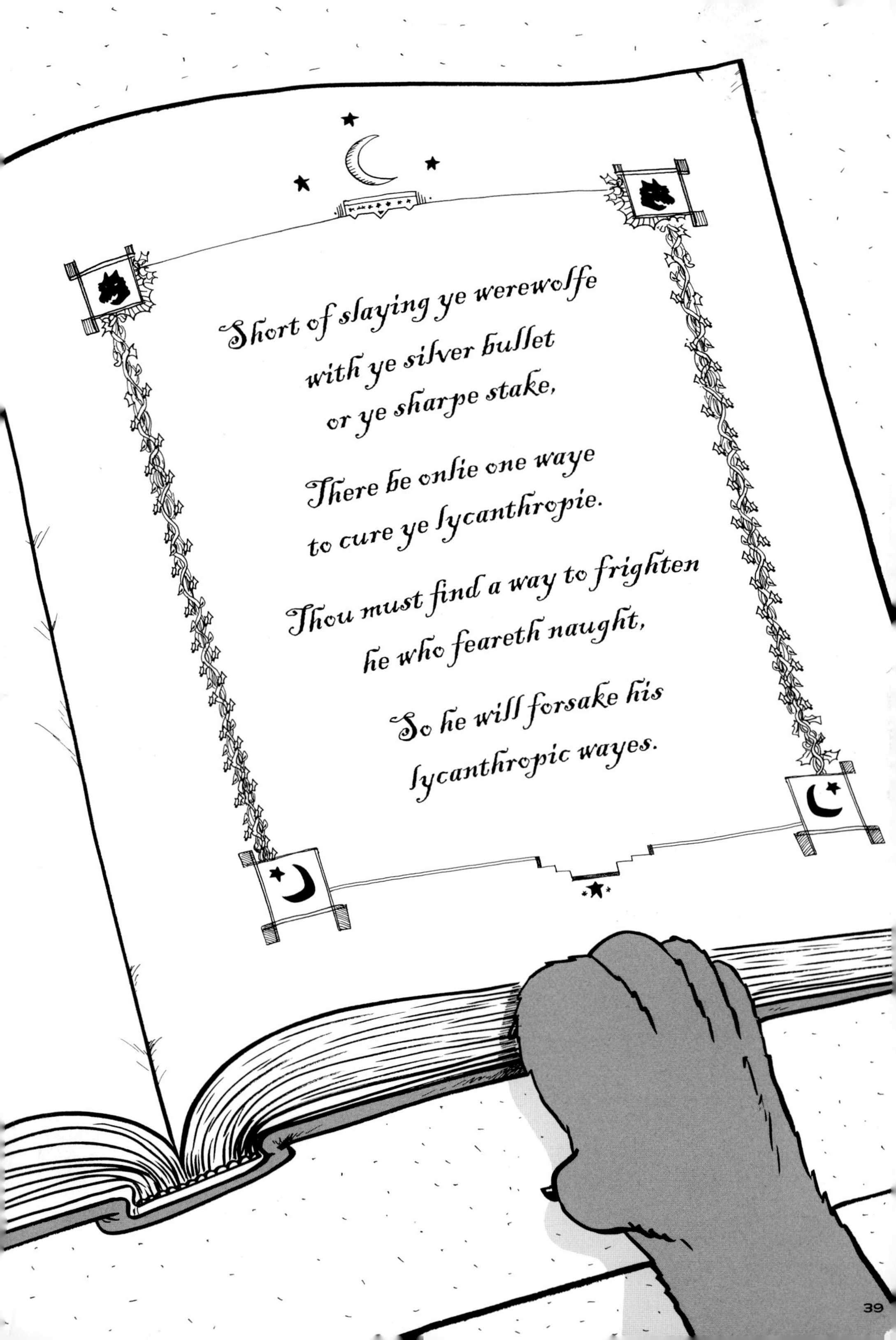
Short of slaying ye werewolfe
with ye silver bullet
or ye sharpe stake,
There be onlie one waye
to cure ye lycanthropie.
Thou must find a way to frighten
he who feareth naught,
So he will forsake his
lycanthropic wayes.

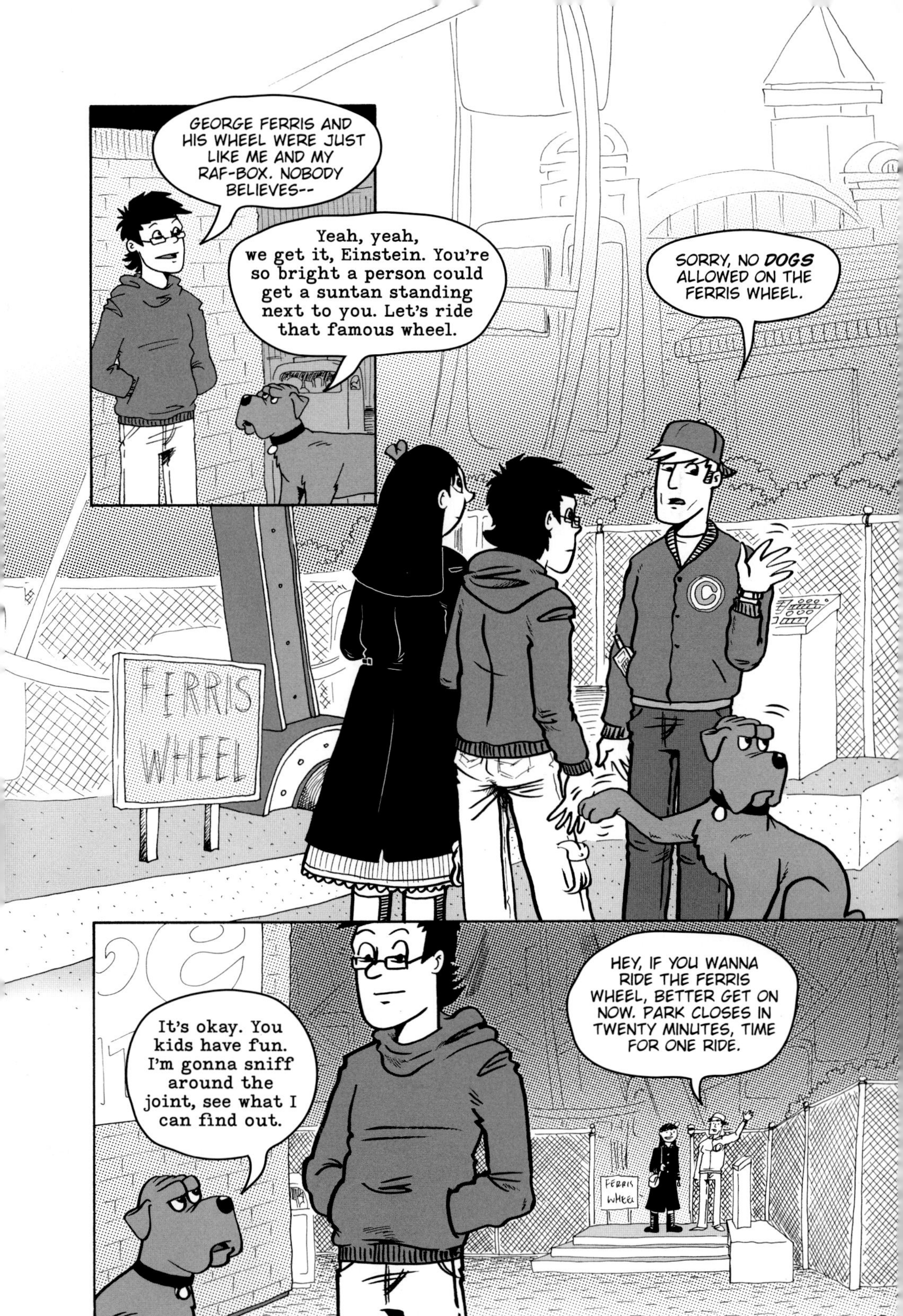
GEORGE FERRIS AND HIS WHEEL WERE JUST LIKE ME AND MY RAF-BOX. NOBODY BELIEVES--
Yeah, yeah, we get it, Einstein. You're so bright a person could get a suntan standing next to you. Let's ride that famous wheel.
SORRY, NO ***DOGS*** ALLOWED ON THE FERRIS WHEEL.
FERRIS WHEEL
It's okay. You kids have fun. I'm gonna sniff around the joint, see what I can find out.
HEY, IF YOU WANNA RIDE THE FERRIS WHEEL, BETTER GET ON NOW. PARK CLOSES IN TWENTY MINUTES, TIME FOR ONE RIDE.

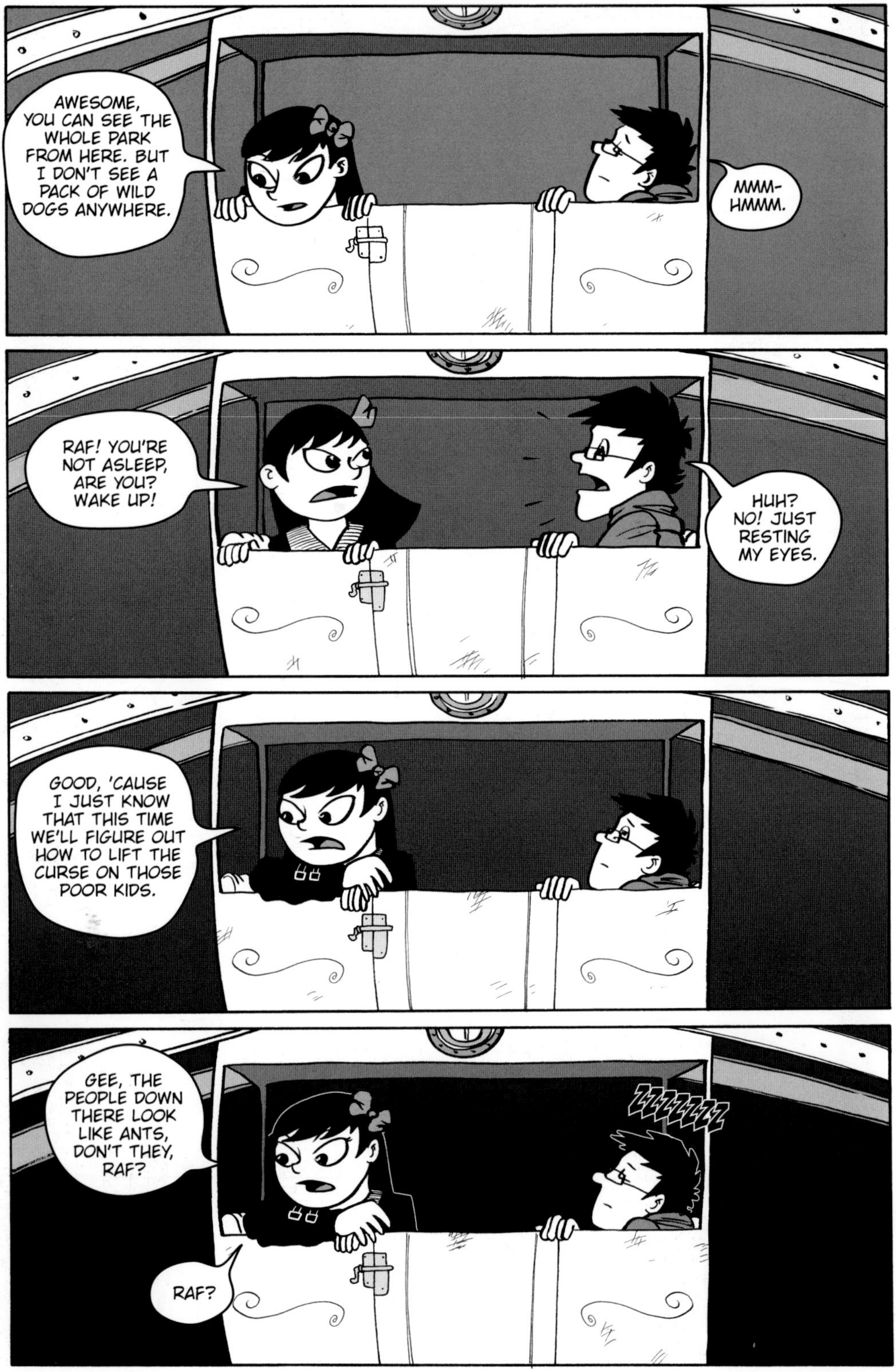
AWESOME, YOU CAN SEE THE WHOLE PARK FROM HERE. BUT I DON'T SEE A PACK OF WILD DOGS ANYWHERE.
MMM-HMMM.
RAF! YOU'RE NOT ASLEEP, ARE YOU? WAKE UP!
HUH? NO! JUST RESTING MY EYES.
GOOD, 'CAUSE I JUST KNOW THAT THIS TIME WE'LL FIGURE OUT HOW TO LIFT THE CURSE ON THOSE POOR KIDS.
GEE, THE PEOPLE DOWN THERE LOOK LIKE ANTS, DON'T THEY, RAF?
ZZZZZZZZ
RAF?

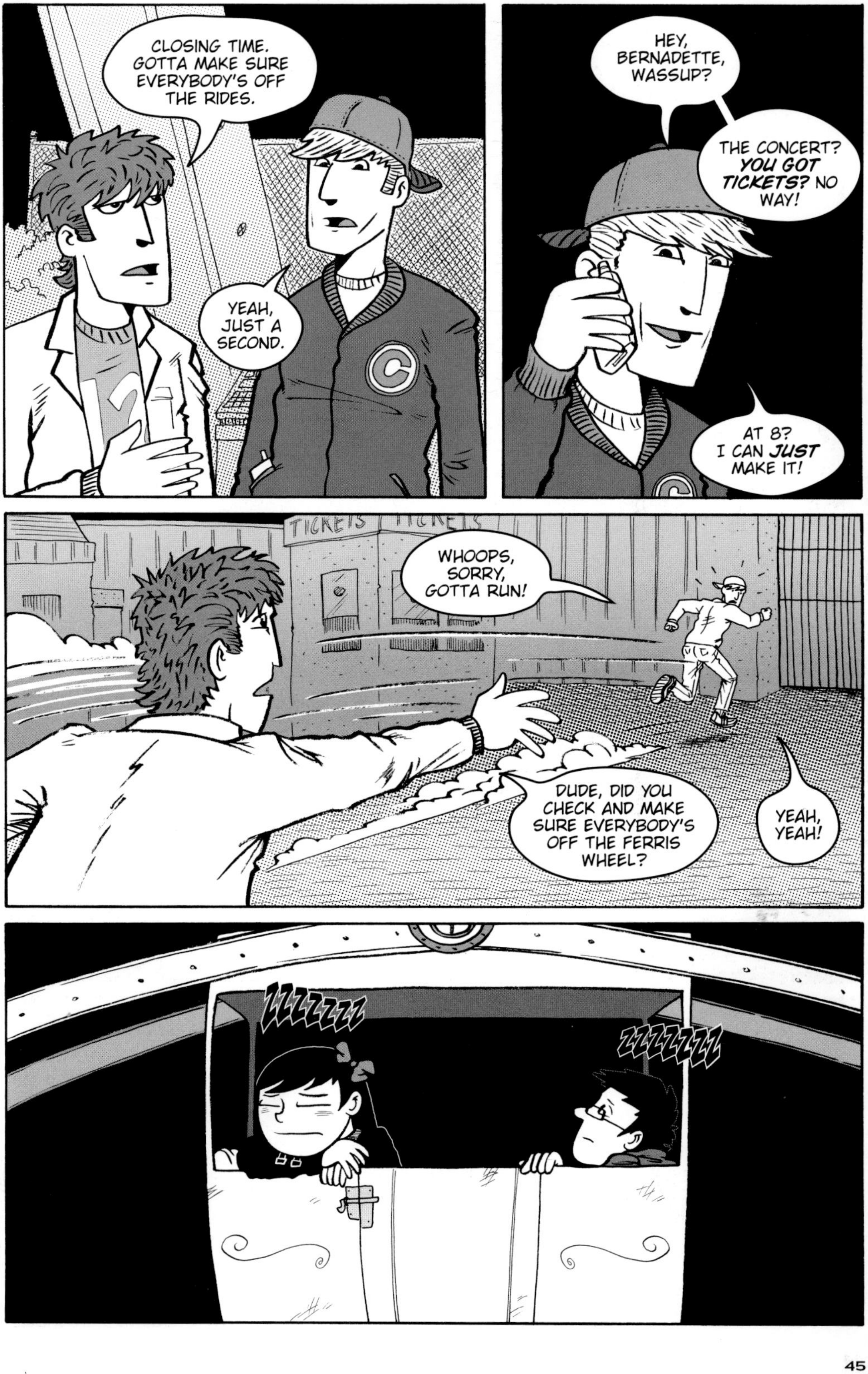
CLOSING TIME. GOTTA MAKE SURE EVERYBODY'S OFF THE RIDES.
YEAH, JUST A SECOND.
HEY, BERNADETTE, WASSUP?
THE CONCERT? YOU GOT TICKETS? NO WAY!
AT 8? I CAN JUST MAKE IT!
TICKETS
TICKETS
WHOOPS, SORRY, GOTTA RUN!
DUDE, DID YOU CHECK AND MAKE SURE EVERYBODY'S OFF THE FERRIS WHEEL?
YEAH, YEAH!
ZZZZZZZ
ZZZZZZZZ

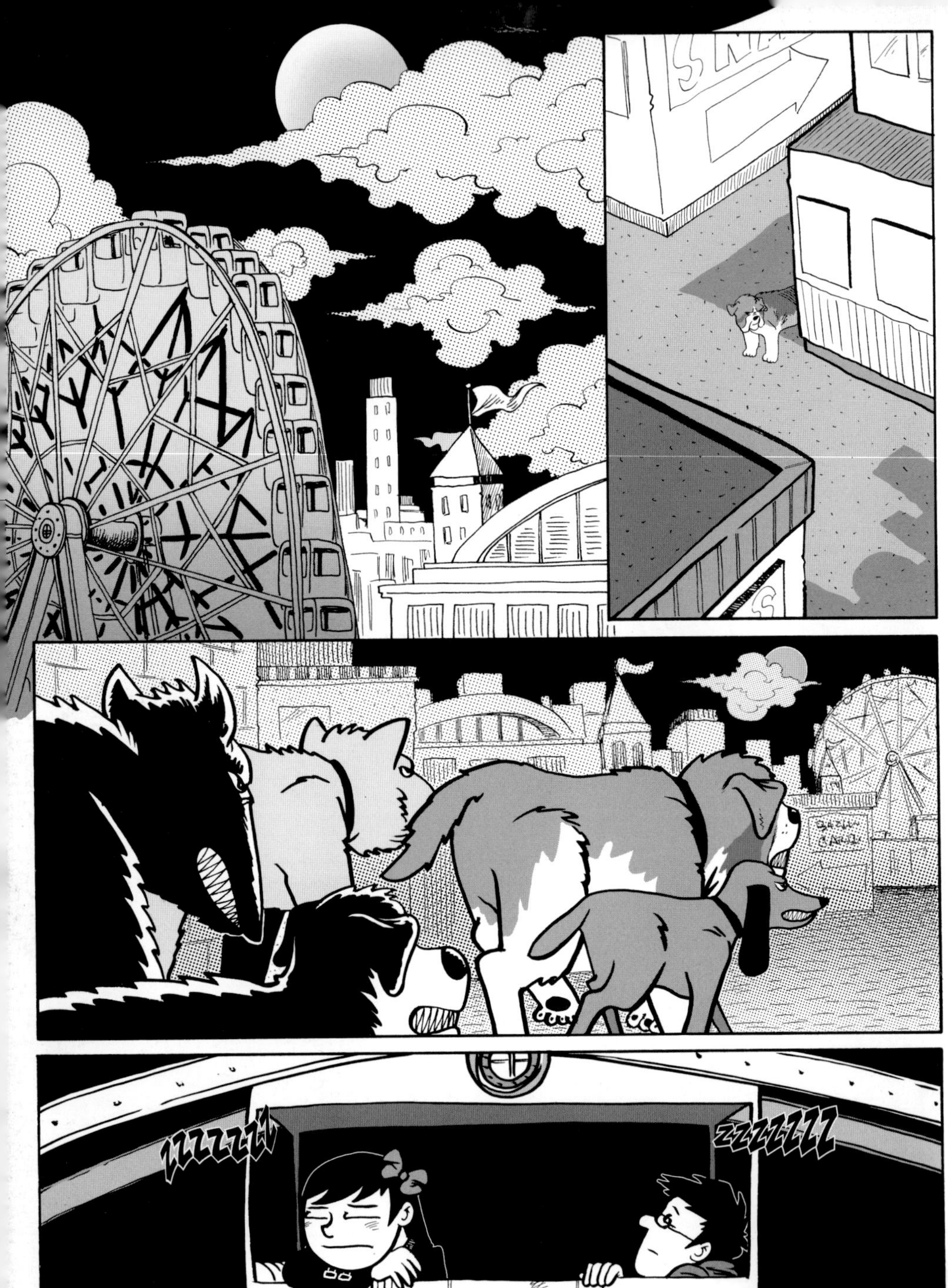
ZZZZZZZ
ZZZZZZZ

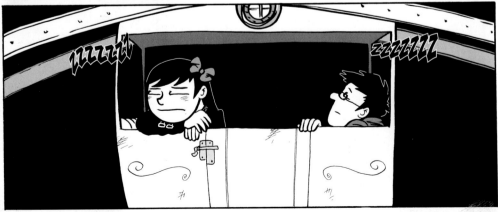

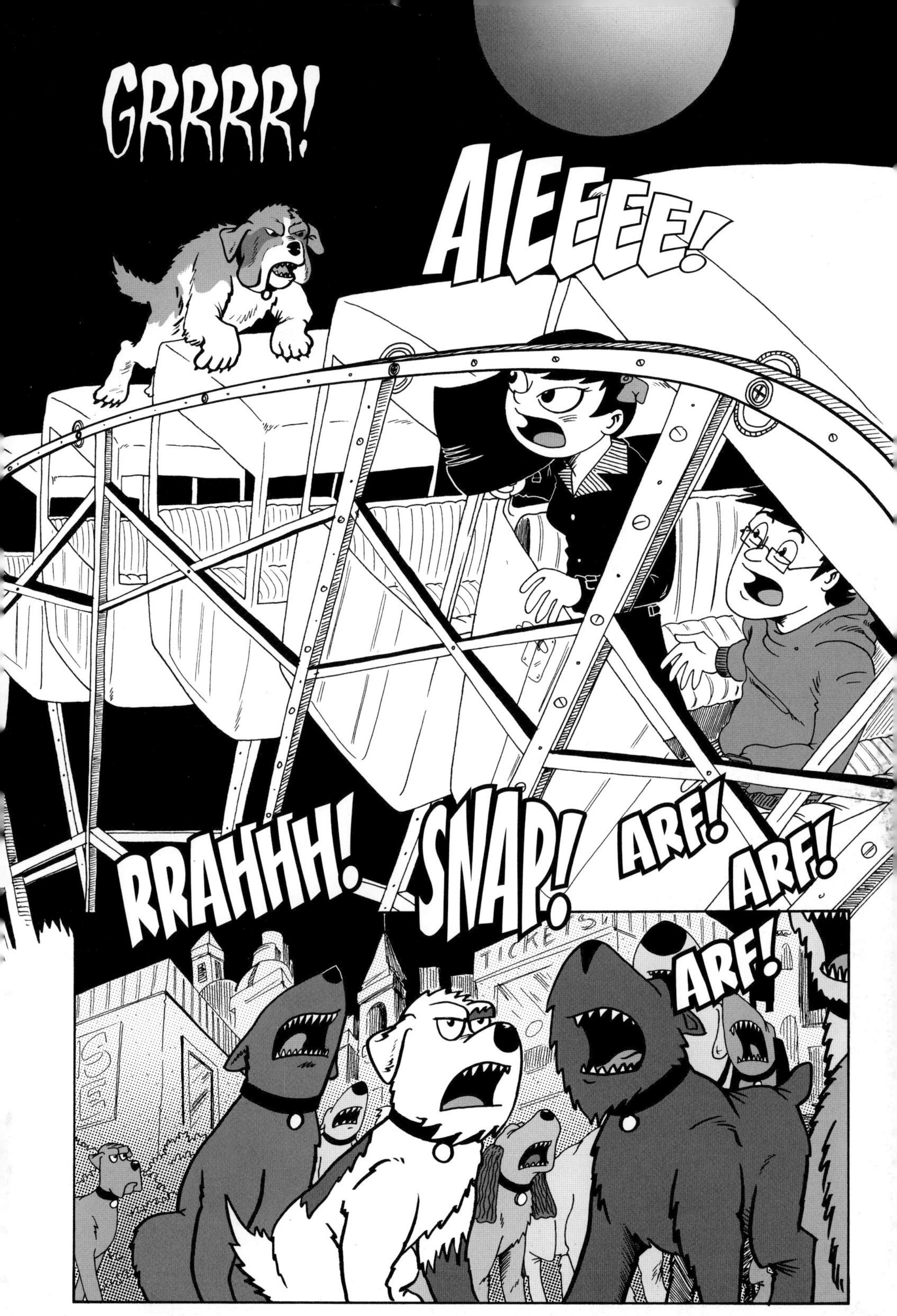
GRRRR!
AIEEEE!
RRAHHH!
SNAP!
ARF!
ARF!
ARF!
TICKETS

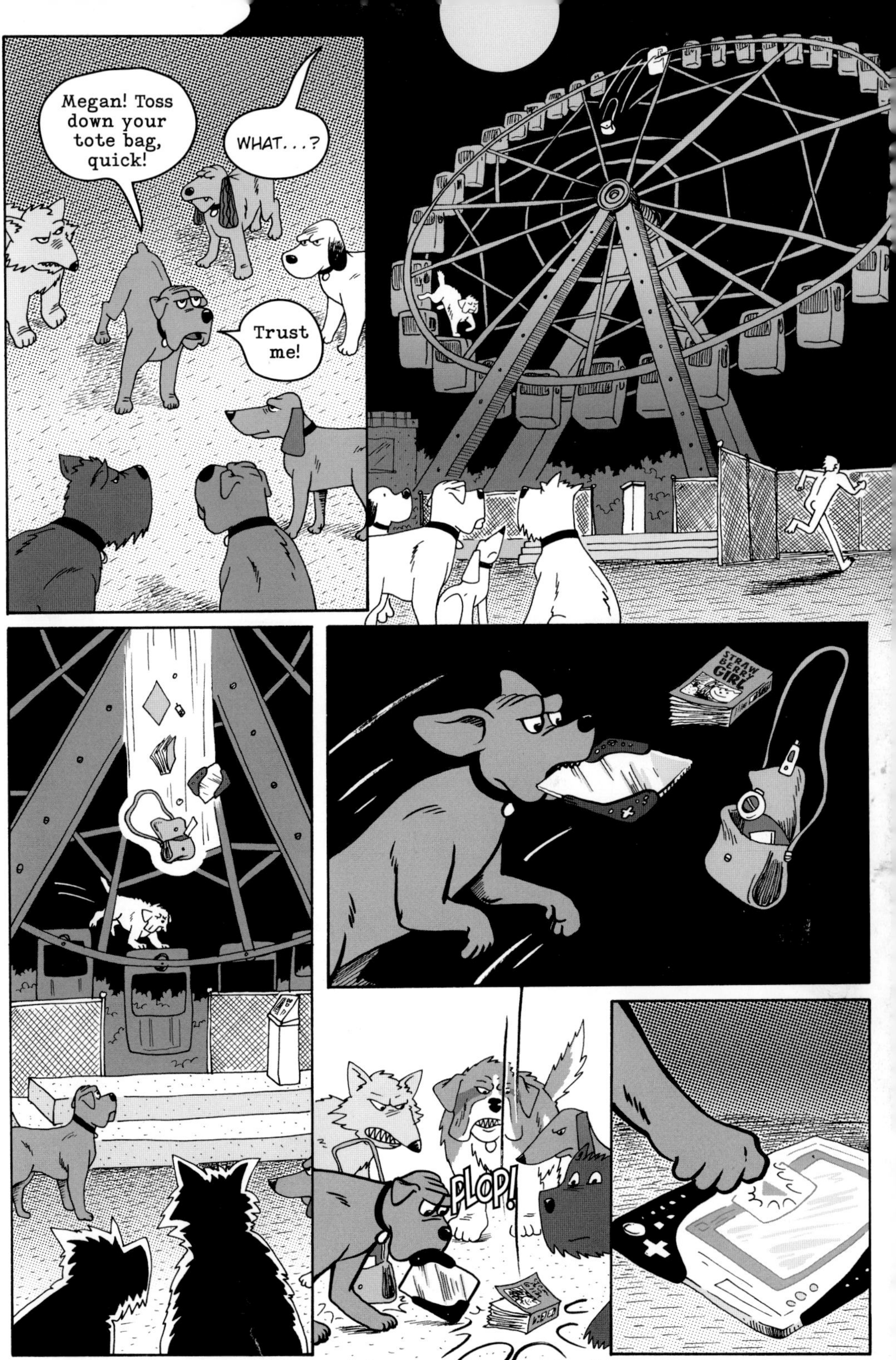
Megan! Toss down your tote bag, quick!
WHAT...?
Trust me!
STRAW BERRY GIRL
PLOP!

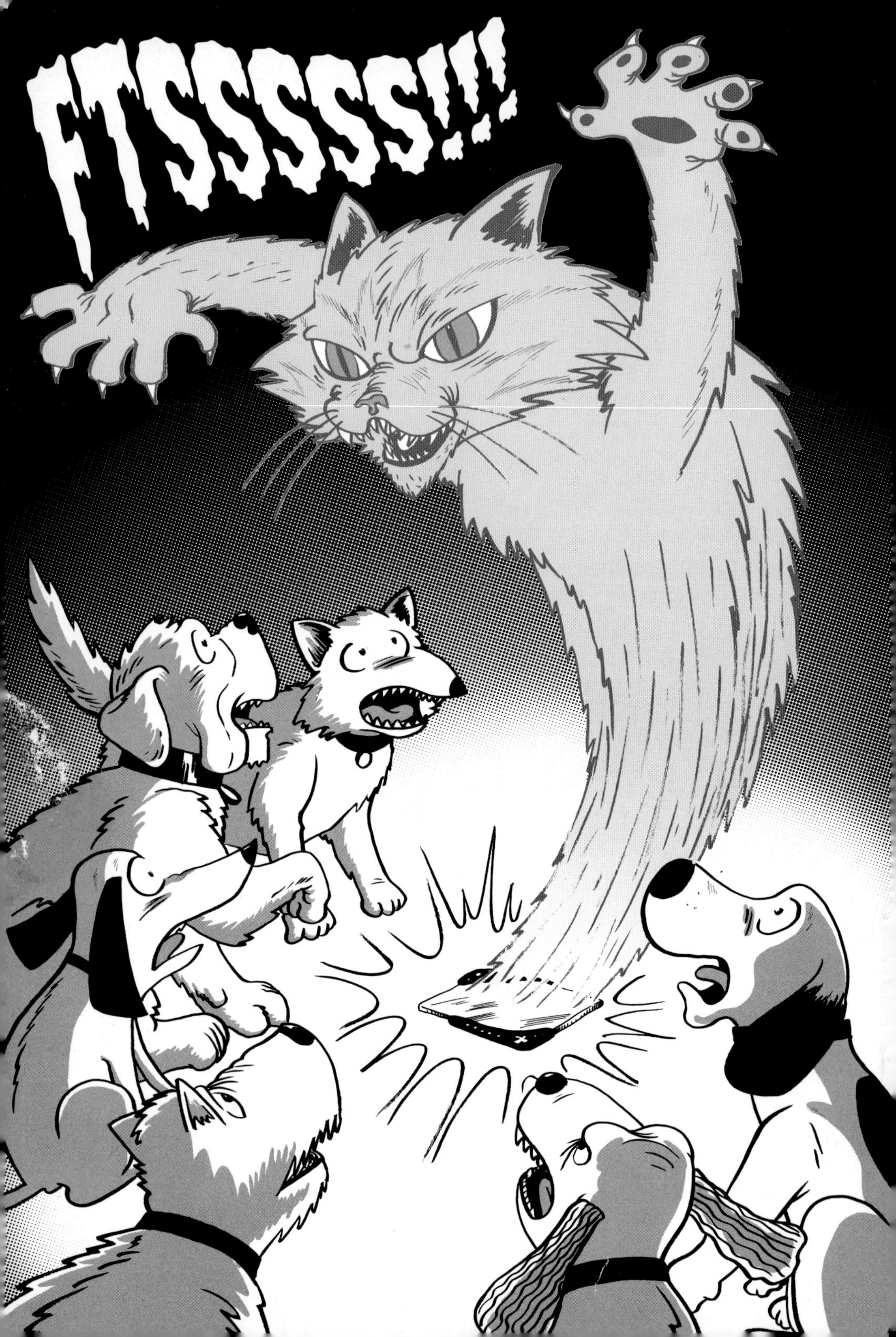
FTSSSSS!!!

EPILOGUE: A NEW LEASH ON LIFE

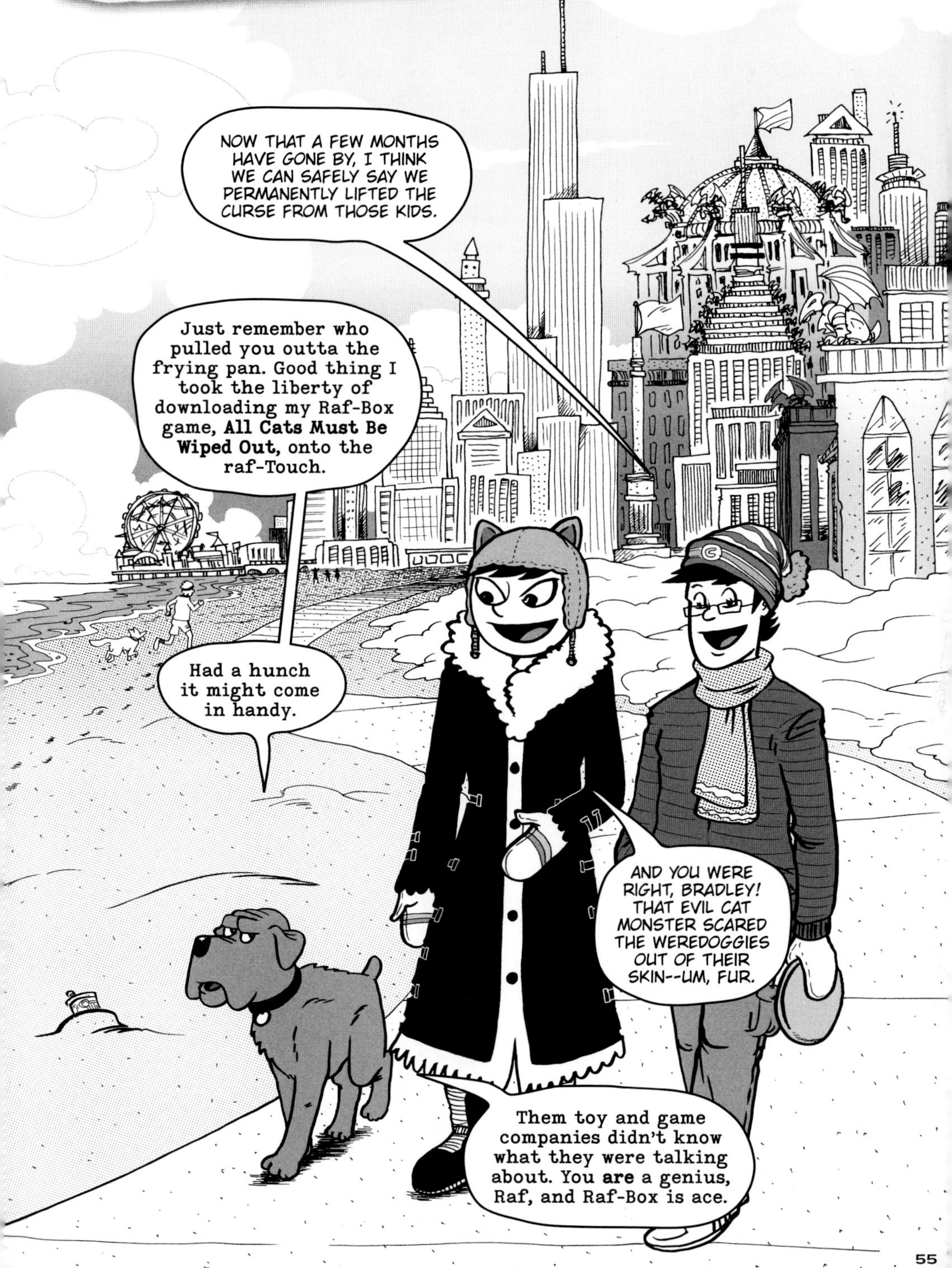
NOW THAT A FEW MONTHS HAVE GONE BY, I THINK WE CAN SAFELY SAY WE PERMANENTLY LIFTED THE CURSE FROM THOSE KIDS.
Just remember who pulled you outta the frying pan. Good thing I took the liberty of downloading my Raf-Box game, **All Cats Must Be Wiped Out,** onto the raf-Touch.
Had a hunch it might come in handy.
AND YOU WERE RIGHT, BRADLEY! THAT EVIL CAT MONSTER SCARED THE WEREDOGGIES OUT OF THEIR SKIN--UM, FUR.
Them toy and game companies didn't know what they were talking about. You **are** a genius, Raf, and Raf-Box is ace.

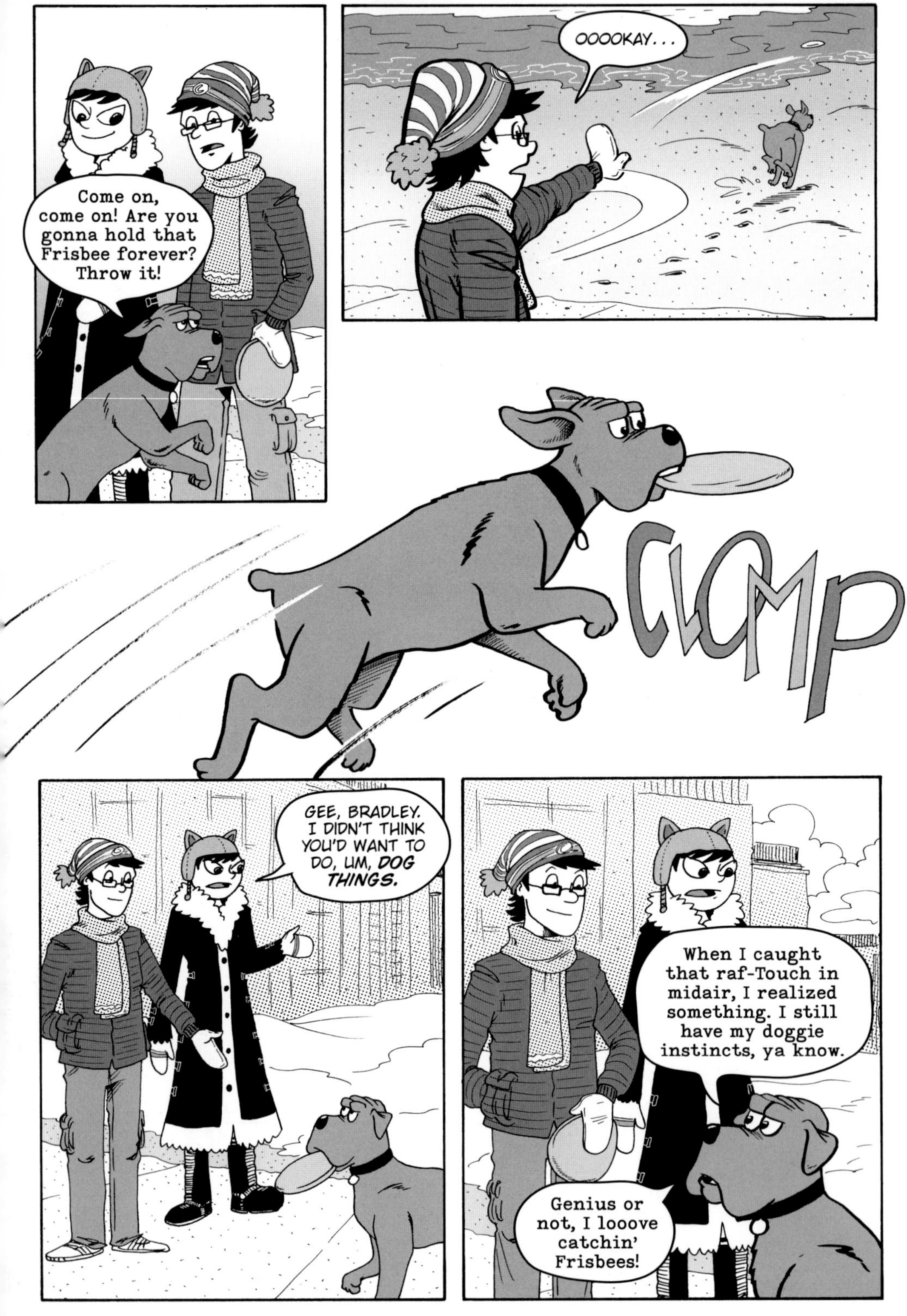
Come on, come on! Are you gonna hold that Frisbee forever? Throw it!
OOOOKAY. . .
CLOMP
GEE, BRADLEY. I DIDN'T THINK YOU'D WANT TO DO, UM, DOG THINGS.
When I caught that raf-Touch in midair, I realized something. I still have my doggie instincts, ya know.
Genius or not, I looove catchin' Frisbees!

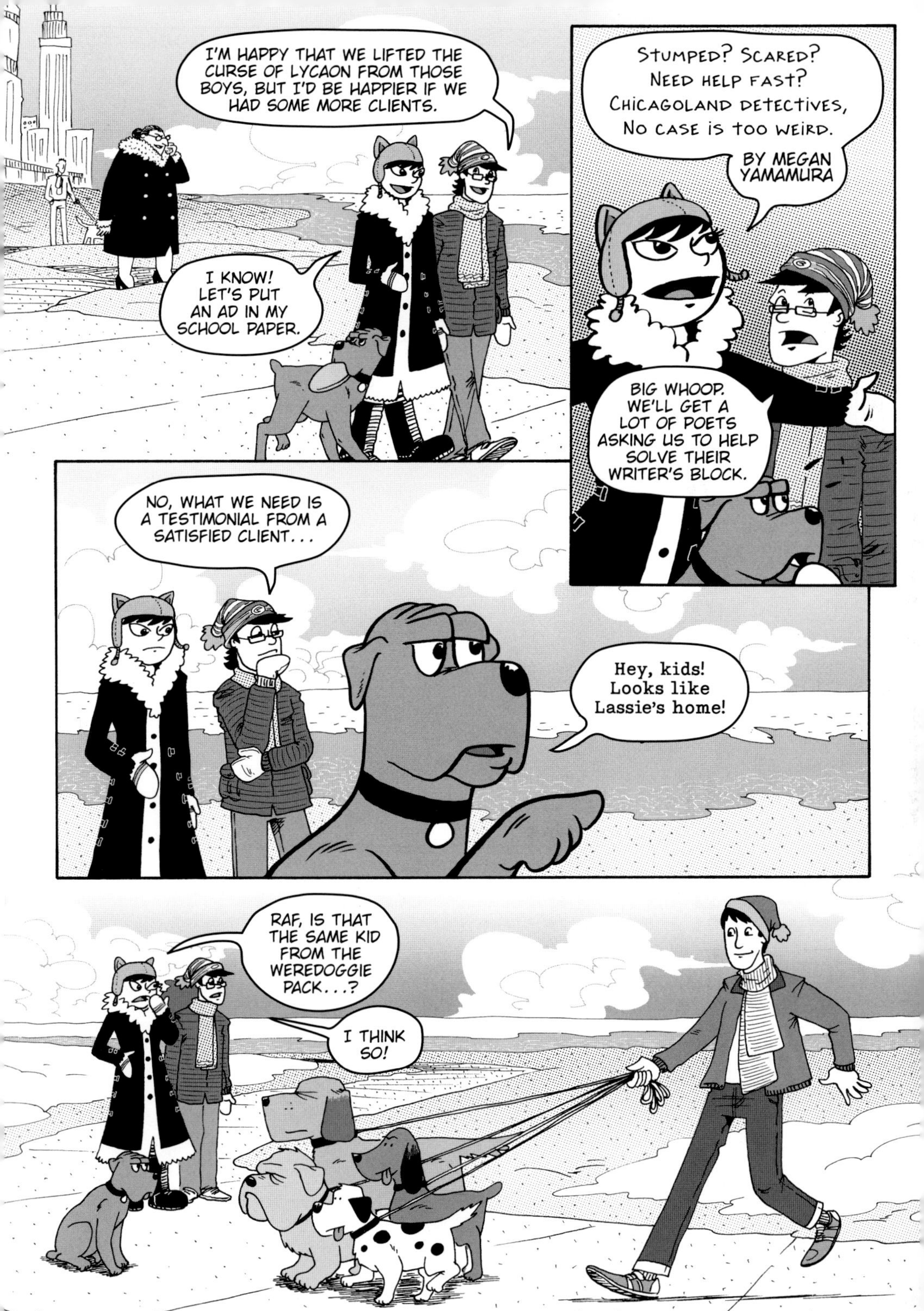
I'M HAPPY THAT WE LIFTED THE CURSE OF LYCAON FROM THOSE BOYS, BUT I'D BE HAPPIER IF WE HAD SOME MORE CLIENTS.
I KNOW! LET'S PUT AN AD IN MY SCHOOL PAPER.
STUMPED? SCARED? NEED HELP FAST? CHICAGOLAND DETECTIVES, NO CASE IS TOO WEIRD.
BY MEGAN YAMAMURA
BIG WHOOP. WE'LL GET A LOT OF POETS ASKING US TO HELP SOLVE THEIR WRITER'S BLOCK.
NO, WHAT WE NEED IS A TESTIMONIAL FROM A SATISFIED CLIENT...
Hey, kids! Looks like Lassie's home!
RAF, IS THAT THE SAME KID FROM THE WEREDOGGIE PACK...?
I THINK SO!

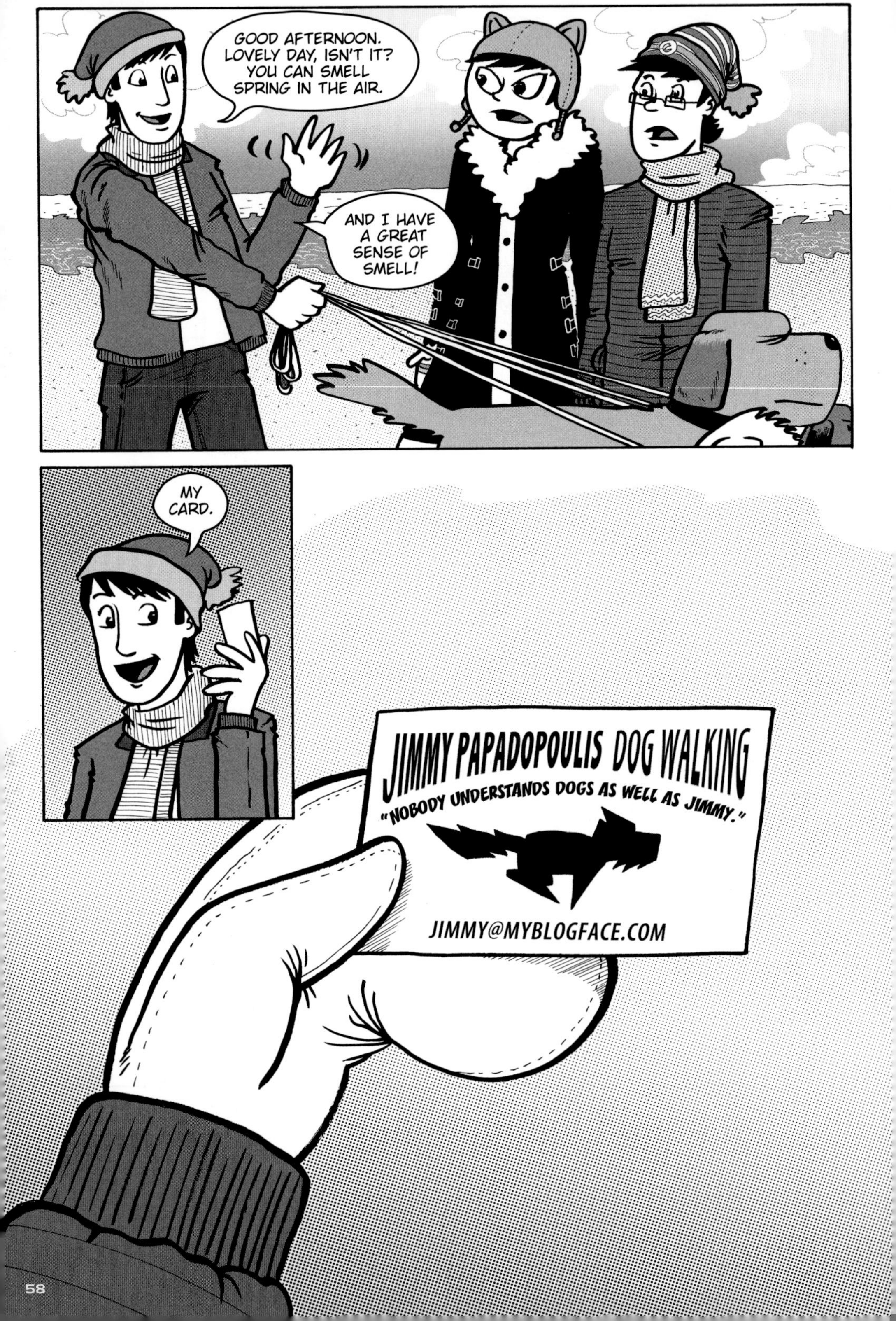
GOOD AFTERNOON. LOVELY DAY, ISN'T IT? YOU CAN SMELL SPRING IN THE AIR.
AND I HAVE A GREAT SENSE OF SMELL!
MY CARD.
JIMMY PAPADOPOULIS DOG WALKING
"NOBODY UNDERSTANDS DOGS AS WELL AS JIMMY."
JIMMY@MYBLOGFACE.COM

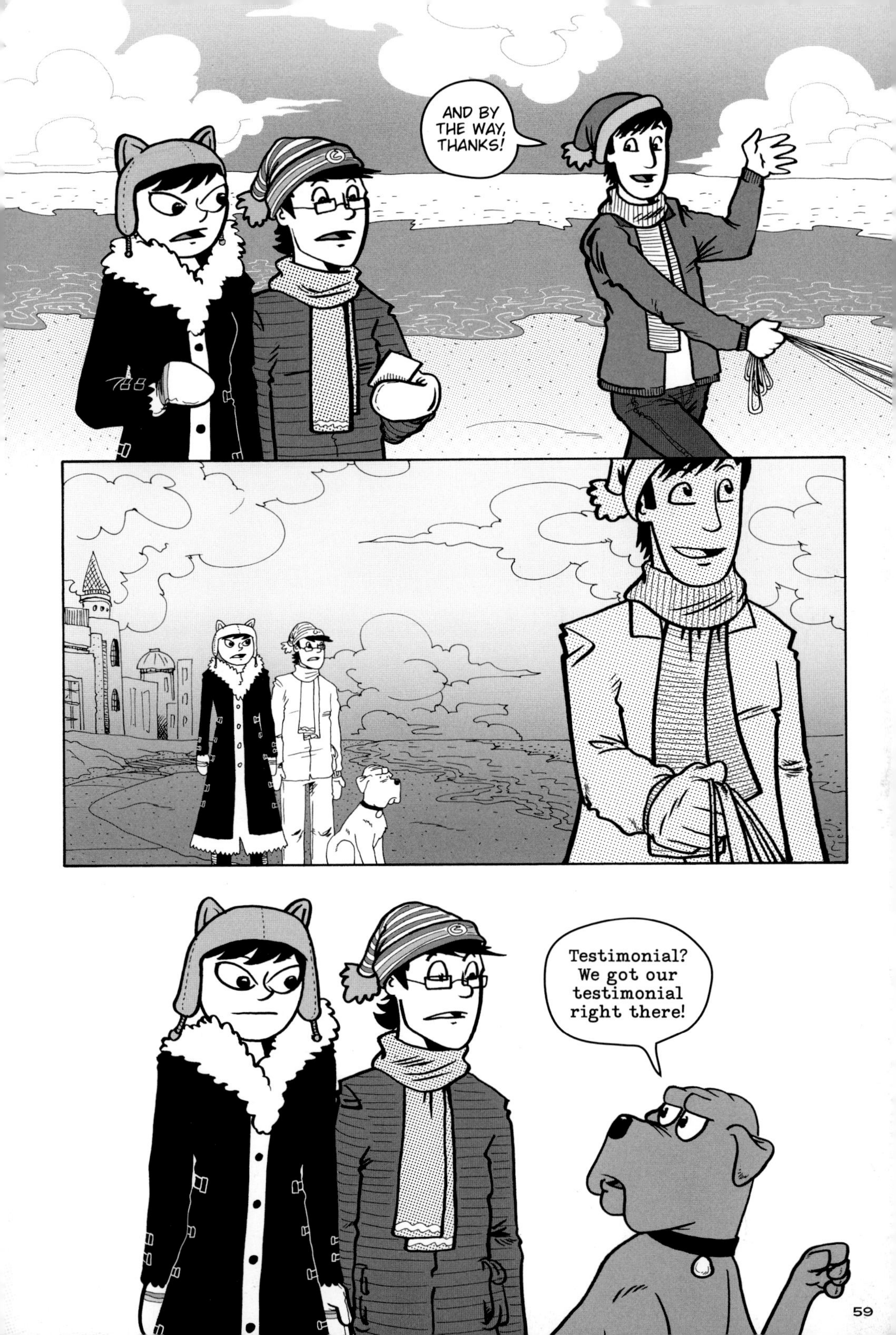
AND BY THE WAY, THANKS!
Testimonial? We got our testimonial right there!

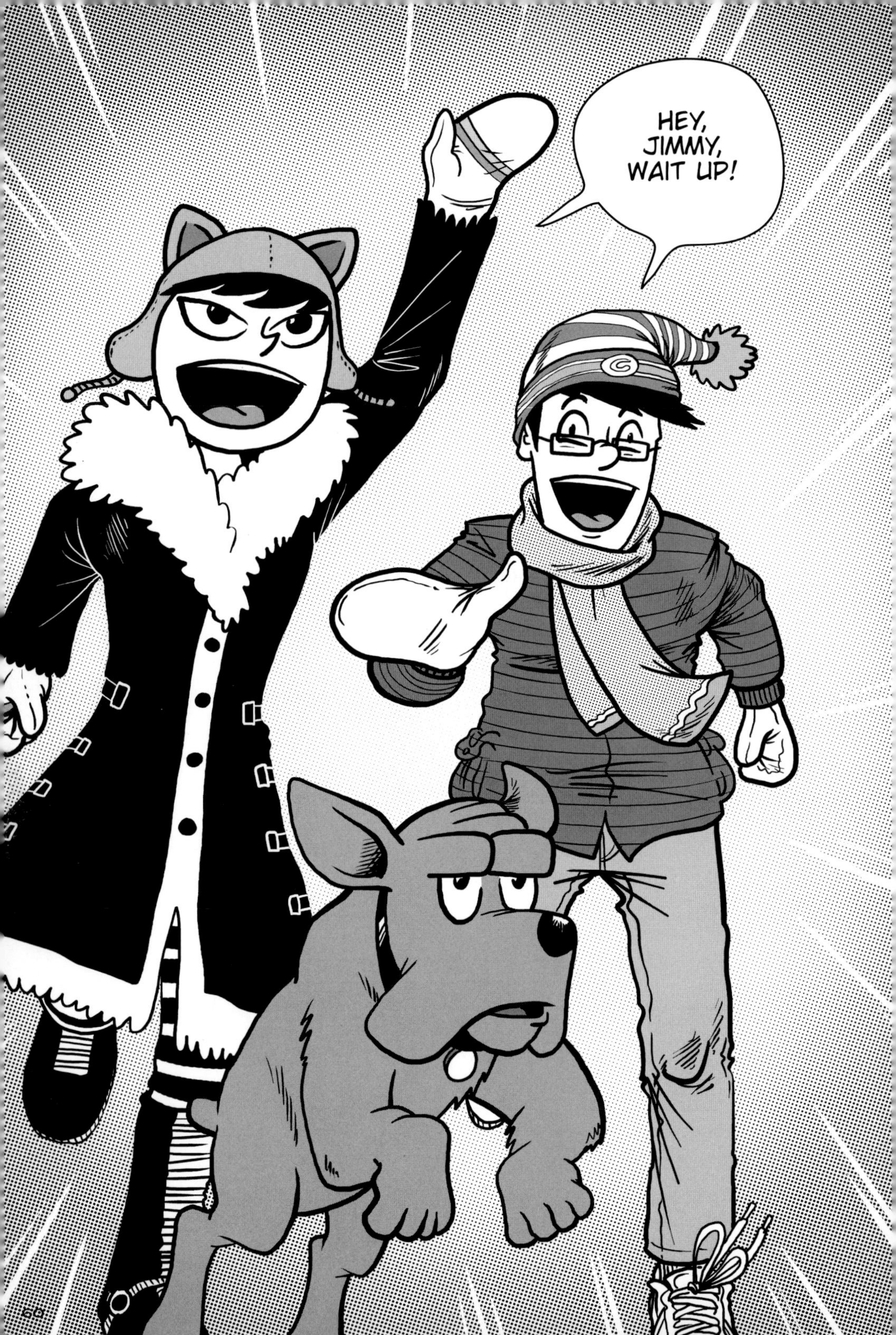
HEY, JIMMY, WAIT UP!

Login: chicagoland

Password: •••••n|

Click here to interFACE

CHICAGOLAND
DETECTIVE AGENCY

Stumped? Scared? Need help fast?
Chicagoland Detectives:
No case is too weird!

The Chicagoland Detective Agency is here for you. We solve low crimes and misdemeanors, and we battle injustice. Don't be afraid to come in with your pets. We love animals.

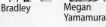

Rhonda Kanaris The Chicagoland Detective Agency did their very best to find out all about the mystery puppy who came to our kitchen door, and even though it turned out that dog was not available for adoption, they inspired us to adopt another puppy. He's so cute!

We adopted him from a rescue group. Rescue groups find foster homes and permanent homes for dogs whose humans have to give them up for some reason, like they're moving to an apartment or they have an allergy. Or if the dogs grow way bigger than the humans understood they would get. Some groups only work with one breed of dog, and some work with mutts (<3 mutts!), and some work with cats. They always educate people on what to expect with a certain type of dog (like whether he's going to grow bigger than my brother Davey).

Rescue groups help take some of the hard work from animal shelters, so we decided to help a rescue group by adopting a puppy from them. And we found a dog that's just right for us.

October 18 at 4:25 PM

Jimmy Papadopoulis Thanks for you-know-what. Dudes you rock!

October 19 at 5:35 PM

Davey Kanaris Yeah right ok. I guess you do rock.

October 19 at 7:13 PM

ABOUT THE AUTHOR AND ILLUSTRATOR

Trina Robbins, an Eisner Award and Harvey Award nominee, made a name for herself in the underground comix movement of the 1960s. She published the first all-woman comic book in the 1970s; published her first history of women cartoonists, *Women and the Comics*, in the 1980s; was an artist for the *Wonder Woman* comic book; and created the superhero series *Go Girl!* with artist Anne Timmons. And that's just a start—she has written biographies, other nonfiction, and way too many other books and comics for kids and adults to list, but you can check them out on her website at www.trinarobbins.com. She lives in San Francisco with her partner, comics artist Steve Leialoha.

Tyler Page is an Eisner Award-nominated illustrator and webcomic artist who has self-published four graphic novels, including *Nothing Better*, recipient of a Xeric Foundation Grant. His day job is director of Print Technology at the Minneapolis College of Art and Design, where he oversees the college's print-based facilities. He's been drawing his whole life and sometime around middle school started making his own comics starring the family cat. He lives with wife Cori Doerrfeld, daughter Charlotte, and two crazy cats in Minneapolis, and his website lives at www.stylishvittles.com.